T0124230

PEACE ON
EARTH

PEACE ON EARTH

R J R

 iUniverse®

PEACE ON EARTH

iUniverse books may be ordered through booksellers or by contacting:

iUniverse
1663 Liberty Drive
Bloomington, IN 47403
www.iuniverse.com
1-800-Authors (1-800-288-4677)

ISBN: 978-1-5320-9492-7 (sc)
ISBN: 978-1-5320-9493-4 (e)

Library of Congress Control Number: 2020910115

Print information available on the last page.

iUniverse rev. date: 06/08/2020

CONTENTS

Chapter 1　The Arrival 1
Chapter 2　The Mission 5
Chapter 3　The Desert 11
Chapter 4　ICE and Stone 21
Chapter 5　Joe Knows 35
Chapter 6　The Story of Pamuhl 47
Chapter 7　Time to Go.. 59
Chapter 8　Gray Area 67
Chapter 9　Bi-Bi 73
Chapter 10　Spaghetti Betty 87
Chapter 11　Return to Sender 93
Chapter 12　Searching Brownywood 107
Chapter 13　Now What? 115
Chapter 14　What about Deltoiga?................................. 125
Chapter 15　I Never Signed Up for This......................... 133
Chapter 16　Have to Eat and Run 143
Chapter 17　What Are We Doing Now? 151

Chapter 18 Moe, Joe, and Cindy.................................... 159
Chapter 19 It's a Long Way to Arizona 167
Chapter 20 Ursa, Nybo, and the Deltoigans.................. 175
Chapter 21 Planning for Trouble.................................... 185
Chapter 22 The Quiet before the Storm......................... 193
Chapter 23 Deep Space... 199
Chapter 24 The War Begins... 211
Chapter 25 Turning Points... 217
Chapter 26 There Is Still Hope 225
Chapter 27 The Vibrator Bomb Is Tested...................... 233
Chapter 28 Nybo versus Will Robinson 241
Chapter 29 Life in the Stone Age 247

CHAPTER 1

THE ARRIVAL

Nybo peeks out of his spacecraft and embraces his first look at the planet United States of America. Stepping out of the craft, he feels the heat of the Arizona desert, which is currently 105 degrees. The weight from deep within his stomach rises, causing him to experience a tickling sensation. He takes a few steps to check the gravity. *Not much*, he thinks. Looking back at his spacecraft, Nybo sees that the vehicle is transparent and appears as heat reflecting off an asphalt highway, invisible to the human eye.

Nybo feels proud for having been selected to make the trip to the planet United States of America. He has traveled deeper into space than any voyager from his planet has ever gone, at least any that ever returned home. He is amazed how the scientists on his planet were able to pinpoint his destination by tracing radio waves back to their source. He wonders how they put him in a meditative, comatose-like state and predetermined exactly when to have him awaken so he could contact loved ones back home and prepare for the arrival.

Nybo is thankful the weather conditions are perfect to telepathically communicate with his wisdom guide for this journey, Albie III, who is back on Deltoiga his home planet. Nybo confirms that the voyage went smoothly and all Albie III's calculations were accurate. Albie III congratulates Nybo and instructs him to begin running the surface test.

After a few moments pass, Nybo informs Albie III, "The gravitational pull is 9.81 m/s^2. That explains the tickling feeling I have."

"That is very close to what we calculated," responds Albie III.

"Lucky guess," states Nybo.

Albie III says, "Don't jump too high without your gravity shoes, or it will take you a half hour to come back down." They chuckle.

Gravity shoes are like magnets. They assist in normalizing the gravitational pull of a planet. The pull of the shoe can be adjusted from weak to extreme. Nybo adjusts his shoes, and the tickling feeling he has been experiencing disappears.

Albie III tells Nybo that it is time to begin his mission. He instructs Nybo to take the form of a USAite, a human being. An image of a USAite once briefly appeared to a few of the leaders on Deltoiga. Nybo stretches and takes the form of the image they had seen. The image was Danny Devito.

At first, the USAite form feels odd, but Nybo soon settles into it. Following a sad farewell to his spacecraft, the trek begins. Facing uncertainty and total aloneness, Nybo walks and reviews the instructions he received about looking, speaking, and acting like a USAite.

After walking a few minutes, Nybo realizes that he does not know where he is going. He stops and looks around. He's suddenly contacted by Albie III, who says, "I sense that you are confused, Nybo. Pick a landmark and go in that direction. Choose something that could be useful in helping you relocate your spacecraft if there's interference with your *jomo*."

Jomo is a sense Deltoigans have. They use it to locate items they have misplaced. At times, windstorms and severe weather can interfere with jomo and render it useless.

So Nybo is on his way. Looking like a human being walking through the desert, wearing funny shoes, he adapts to USAite form with every step.

THE MISSION

Deltoiga is a small, undiscovered planet far across the multiverse. Deltoigans are happy by nature. Some of them do not even know what sadness is. They are like members of an ant colony or beehive. Everyone does the right thing. They do whatever is necessary for the good of the community without knowing or caring why.

The citizens of Deltoiga rarely speak to one another. It is not that they are angry or cannot speak—it just is not necessary. Almost all communication on Deltoiga is done telepathically. Deltoigans have learned to keep their thoughts respectful since you can never be sure who might be receiving them. It is not nice to have thoughts about others behind their backs. No one wants to be known as a gossip thinker.

There is a governing committee on Deltoiga called the Wisdom Core. The head of the Wisdom Core is the Wisdom Supreme, a senior member of the Wisdom Core who has demonstrated exceptional telepathic abilities and who has been proven to make sound decisions on difficult issues. The Wisdom Core meets randomly, only when it is deemed necessary by the Wisdom Supreme.

The Wisdom Core meetings are held in the sacred Cave of Wisdom. The walls of the cave are thick enough to keep the thoughts being generated in the cave from leaking outside, not that anyone cares. As you can imagine, there are very few secrets on Deltoiga. The walls of the cave are needed to keep thoughts from the outside on the outside so they do not interfere with the meetings. The cave is small, and if you listen closely, you can hear thoughts echoing off the walls.

About a year ago, a meeting was called by the Wisdom Supreme to discuss messages being received from a planet called the United States of America. The Wisdom Supreme was the first to hear them. He repeatedly received a message for almost two years before anyone else heard it. The message was always the same. It said, "This is the United States of America. Is anyone out there?"

Since the Wisdom Supreme had begun receiving the message before everybody else, they started to believe that he was losing his marbles. He began to receive snickering thoughts as people passed by. Things like, *Heard from America lately?* or, *Too bad about your marbles. Lose any today?* But then others began to receive the message as well.

One day, different messages began to be received. Some Deltoigans heard one message, and others heard another. Different messages were randomly coming in, and not everyone was receiving the same ones. These messages were high-frequency radio waves from radio shows and audio from television shows that had escaped the earth's ionosphere. Unaware of Earth, Deltoigans believed the messages were coming from the planet United States of America. One day, a brief visual image came to a few Wisdom Core members—the Danny Devito image, the form Nybo would take. So it was time for a meeting of the Wisdom Core, the first one in over a year.

The first part of the meeting went routinely smooth. All but two members were present. One of them was protesting what he felt was a lack of interest that his thoughts had been receiving lately from the group. The other was unable to think or communicate clearly since the lab explosion. He had been working on a new form of energy when a careless lab assistant knocked over a vat in the laboratory, causing an explosion. The explosion created a great vibration that then caused the brain of everyone in the lab to rattle. Seven Deltoigans in all were affected. It was estimated that their thoughts would return to normal in a month or two, as the vibration should be done by then.

The meeting proceeded quietly since it was all done telepathically. The Wisdom Core unanimously decided that a voyage to the planet United States of America was necessary. The first part of the mission would be to inform the leader of the planet United States of America that the voyager Anyone had not been seen or heard from by the Deltoigans. Anyone was obviously still missing since they continued to look for him.

The second part of the mission was to see if the planet United States of America had seen or heard from any of Deltoiga's missing voyagers. Communication had been lost with four voyagers from Deltoiga over the last twenty years. The United States of America must be highly advanced in voyaging, so perhaps they could help find them. All Wisdom

Core members silently cheered, and you could feel the excitement in the air.

The trouble started during the discussion of which voyager should be appointed to take the mission. There were several able and deserving candidates suggested. Nybo was not one of them.

Each member of the Wisdom Core suggested the name of a voyager who they thought would be best for the mission. With each suggestion given, others reacted, some supportive, some not. About halfway through the suggestions, some of the reactions turned negative. Tension began to rise as more and more members had their recommendations challenged by the other members. Tension interferes with the ability to receive messages. You cannot always be sure who is sending a thought. This soon became the situation at the meeting.

Member Expador was thinking to the committee when unidentified interruptions began to occur—negative, snickering thoughts that were the cause of a telepathic free-for-all. The first interruptive thought Expador received was, *You possess* rare *intelligence. It's* rare *that you show it.*

Expador did his best to let it go and concentrate on supporting his recommendation, only to be interrupted seconds later with, *You know the drill. Send a message, and I ignore it.*

This was followed by chuckling from a few of the other members who had also received it. Expador was getting a little worked up. He attempted to ease the tension by thinking, *Okay, now you're just getting smart.*

Someone responded, *How you would know?* And then, yikes, the whole meeting went silently berserk.

Expador reacted by thinking, *Remember when I asked for your opinion? Me neither.*

Someone responded, *You can't think that.*

Someone else replied, *Whatever makes you stupid really works.*

Expador thought firmly, *Don't you raise your thoughts to me.*

Another unidentified thought was, *If ignorance is bliss, you must be very happy.*

The last straw came when someone thought, *Expador, I would like to help you out. Which way did you come in?*

And then—

"*Stop!*" the Wisdom Supreme stated very sternly. This was the first word orally spoken on Deltoiga in over five months. You could have heard a pin drop, which was no big deal on Deltoiga. The Wisdom Core members were both shocked and embarrassed as they sat motionless in their seats. The Wisdom Supreme went back to communicating telepathically.

Enough, he thought to the committee. *You have all made excellent recommendations of voyagers who are worthy of this mission. I would like to make a recommendation of someone who hasn't been thought of.*

After a brief pause, the Wisdom Supreme thought the name Nybo.

Again, you could have heard a pin drop. And again, no big deal on Deltoiga. The Wisdom Core members began to squirm and fidget in their seats while they attempted to contain their thoughts. Finally, a thought was released.

Nybo?

Others began thinking the same thing. *Nybo? He barely passed voyager school. He spent too much time thinking like a clown and disrupting classes.*

Yes. And don't forget what a vandal he was growing up— toilet-papering the Edelsons' house and going on people's porches and lighting bags of lab waste on fire, then ringing the doorbell and running off to hide. People's shoes glowed so bright they had to throw them away and get new ones. His father's shoe business had record sales during those formative years.

The Wisdom Supreme thought, *Members of the Wisdom Core, please hear me out. Yes, Nybo is a screw-up of a Deltoigan. It isn't common knowledge, but he was the one who threw the Deltoigan-looking dummy in front of the land-rover bus, causing it to stop so fast three Deltoigans had brain rattle for a month. The land-rover driver was so shaken up he had to retire to a desk job. And that's exactly why we should send Nybo.*

The Wisdom Core members became confused.

The Wisdom Supreme continued. *Consider this. He did pass voyager school. Yes, I know he graduated bottom of his class, but he's still a voyager. This mission involves risk. We have lost communication with four of our best voyagers over the last twenty years. Do we really feel comfortable with possibly losing another? Nybo is capable of this, or at least, we hope he is. The loss of another voyager would be devastating. The loss of Nybo … not so bad.*

After very little time and thought discussion, it was decided that Nybo would take the mission.

CHAPTER 3

THE DESERT

Nybo sees a mesa on the horizon and begins walking toward it. After walking for over two hours, he feels the heat of the desert penetrating his shoes. It does not affect him as it would a human being. Deltoigans have a camel-like quality. They can go for up to a week without water. In addition to having an extra layer of fat that stores moisture and releases it as needed, they do not perspire or exhale moisture.

As the temperature climbs to 108 degrees, he looks out at an expanse of dried and cracked clay with red rocks scattered about. There is nothing else to see other than an occasional thorny cholla pod.

It reminds him of the time he was sent to the moon called Nock as a boy. Nock is a tiny moon of Deltoiga with next to nothing on it. It is used as a juvenile punishment center. Nybo was sent there after pulling a string of pranks. The last straw came when he hung a Deltoigan-looking dummy from a tree in the Edelsons' backyard. Mrs. Edelson fainted when she saw it, thinking it was an actual Deltoigan child.

He was sent to Nock for three weeks. There was another boy there too. The two of them were sentenced to flip a six-foot, seventy-pound log around the circumference of the moon. They had to lift one end, stand it on end, and then push it over. Repeat, repeat, repeat for three weeks.

As Nybo continues walking, he recognizes how excited and full of anticipation he feels. *Me, Nybo*, he thinks, *walking on the planet United States of America. I hope I'm lucky enough to encounter a USAite.*

Nybo reaches the mesa and decides that climbing it would give him a better view. Perhaps, he will see a city like Chicago, Houston, or Titusville. Maybe Las Vegas. "Viva Las Vegas, baby," he says to himself while quoting a radio wave he once received.

As he follows a ledge that winds around the perimeter of the mesa, he wonders what they are doing back home on Deltoiga. If it is Saturday, they're probably betting on the *ziphop* races. Going to the ziphop races is like going to a horse track. As he reaches the top of the mesa, he reminisces about the best day he ever had at the ziphop races, but suddenly, his thoughts stop, and his heart sinks. As he looks in all directions, he does not see a city. He does not see anything different other than a few petrified trees half buried in sand.

As he is about to begin the descent back down the mesa, he spots something just beyond the petrified trees. Nybo is unable to distinguish what it might be and decides he will investigate. He approaches the petrified trees at a rapid pace. Once he reaches them, he slows his pace. He is very nervous, both excited and scared at the same time.

Nybo slows down to a crawl as he inches his way toward the object. His heart is beating so hard he is sure it can be heard from several yards away. A shock runs through his body as he suddenly realizes it is dressed like a USAite. The USAite is lying on his side with his back toward Nybo. He is wearing jeans, a long-sleeved T-shirt, and a hat.

Nybo thinks, *Okay, this is it. My first contact with a USAite.* He thinks back to the many briefings he had with Albie III when preparing for the mission. They had gathered all the messages everybody had received and tried to decipher the words so Nybo would be able to communicate. He practiced orally speaking English daily until his jaws ached. And now here he is, suddenly not feeling as confident about his English as he had only moments ago. He begins to doubt himself.

Almost too scared to move, he thinks about how it will be okay. Albie III said he believed USAites are the nicest people in their universe. He said they want aliens to come. They need aliens to come. Aliens are good for the economy, whatever that is.

Nybo continues to try and build his confidence but is still too scared to speak. He begins to feel ill and weak in the knees. *I must speak*, he thinks. *The reason I'm here is to speak. Come on, Nybo. Grow a pair. This whole mission is about speaking.*

I can't do it. What if I blow it? Still full of fear, he thinks, *I must speak. If I don't speak, I can never go back to Deltoiga. I would always be looked at as a failure. I would be the laughingstock of the planet. I would be known as Nybo the chicken. I don't even know what that means, but I don't like it. I couldn't live like that.*

You can do this, Nybo, he thinks as he takes a hard swallow. Following a deep breath, and without being aware he is doing it, he speaks. "Hello, I'm Nybo of Deltoiga."

There is no response. Nybo's thoughts race through his head. *Did I say that wrong? I'm sure I said that right.* He tries again. "Hello, I'm Nybo of Deltoiga. I have come to speak to you about Anyone."

Again, there is no response. Nybo is now confused. After introducing himself for a third time with no response, he realizes that he is getting nowhere with the attempted conversation. He walks around to face the USAite, and with a shock, he exclaims, "Whoa."

It is not a USAite at all. Nybo has found the skeletal remains of an illegal immigrant who got lost trying to cross the desert. As Nybo wonders what it is, he suddenly breaks out laughing. *Of course*, he thinks. *It's a dummy made by some USAite kids. I think I'm really going to like it here.*

Nybo walks for three hours before spotting a palo verde tree in the distance. He walks another half hour before reaching it. Arriving at the tree, he finds clothes and backpacks strewn about, things left behind by exhausted, dehydrated illegal immigrants who no longer had the energy to carry extra items. There are empty black jugs everywhere.

Nybo decides that someone must live here and he will wait a while to see if they come home. As night approaches, Nybo decides he will stay and rest until morning. He takes off his gravity shoes and sets the magnetic pull to full strength. Deltoigan voyagers are trained to do this whenever they take their shoes off, so they will not float away while the voyager is resting.

Nybo sits against the tree and wonders if his English will be any good or if he will even have an opportunity to use it. He looks at the clear night sky and stares at the shinning stars, thinking about how many unknown inhabited planets there must be. *A lot*, he concludes, *since the United States of America is asking aliens to come.*

Nybo relaxes and thinks about Deltoiga. As he wonders why he was the voyager chosen for this mission, he is startled by a noise. He looks out into the darkness and sees movement.

Suddenly, a voice comes from behind him. "Hola, amigo. I'm Miguel."

If Nybo wasn't still sitting, he would have jumped higher than the tree.

"Mind if we share your oasis?"

Turning to see a short, dark-skinned man with black hair, Nybo smiles and nods. Albie III had instructed him to smile and nod whenever he does not understand something.

Nybo is not as nervous about speaking as he was earlier. He does not have time to think about it. He answers, "I'm Nybo of Deltoiga."

"Nice to meet you, Nyboa," says Miguel.

Before Nybo can correct him, the others arrive to the tree, a group of six total. While Nybo is thinking that he has at last met some USAites, Miguel introduces him to the group, "This is Nyboa Deltoiga."

The others are excited and encouraged to meet someone. They tell Nybo that they were part of a much larger group, but ICE came along, and everyone scattered. "We were all separated and lucky to find each other. We don't know what happened to the rest of the group. Some were surely arrested. We have been wandering ever since, not sure if we are even going the right way. Our supplies are very limited."

They begin to ask Nybo questions. "Have you come far?"

Nybo replies, "Yes."

"Has your journey been difficult?"

Nybo replies, "Not really."

"Did you come over the fence or under it?"

"Over it," replies Nybo.

"So you are an alien," says Miguel.

Nybo panics as he wonders what is wrong with his USAite form. What made it so easy to identify him? "What gave it away?" he asks.

"Hey, amigo, we are all aliens. Just trying to settle in the United States and make a better life for our families," answers Miguel.

Nybo is disappointed that the group is made up of aliens and not USAites, but he is glad to make friends. The bomb drops as Miguel asks, "Have you seen anyone?"

Nybo is stunned. "No, I haven't," he says, "but that's why I'm here."

"That's right," says Miguel. "You see ICE, and it's over."

Nybo remembers a PBS signal he once received about the polar ice caps melting and says, "Ice in this heat? It would melt faster than the polar ice caps."

"That's funny, amigo," says Miguel, "but you watch yourself. ICE can be behind any rock or tree."

Nybo looks behind the tree and shrugs his shoulders. The exhausted group turns in for the night. Nybo sits against the tree, too excited to sleep. A woman comes and sits next to him. She introduces herself as Maria and says, "You know, Nyboa, it isn't safe to travel by yourself. There are a lot of bad people out there."

Nybo thinks that maybe he was lucky to have successfully made it to the United States of America. He thinks that he had to travel alone, since to travel comfortably there's only room for one in the spacecraft.

Maria tells Nybo this is her third attempt to come to the United States. She says, "I'd been living in the United States for six years. I was working two jobs. I bought a house."

Nybo smiles and nods.

She continues. "I went back to Mexico for my father's funeral. After two weeks, when I tried to return, they wouldn't allow me through the port of entry."

Nybo thinks, *So she's from a planet called Mexico.*

Maria goes on. "I tried a different port of entry but was denied there also. Finally, after a month I paid a coyote three thousand dollars to smuggle me in. There were about twenty of us in a group. No sooner had we reached the United States when a group of banditos showed up. They took everything— all our items, our water, even our shoes and belts. The coyote left with them. The whole thing was a setup. We had no choice but to return to Mexico."

Nybo smiles and nods.

Maria continues. "So this time I paid five thousand dollars to a coyote. We were separated after the ICE raid, and here I am."

Nybo smiles and nods.

While the others are sleeping, Nybo contacts Albie III. "So good to hear from you Nybo. How did the first day go?"

Nybo excitedly reports, "I have met some aliens from other planets. Planets called El Salvador, Guatemala, and Mexico. Mexico is the main planet. They all travel there first since Mexico has ports of entry to the United States of America. They all refer to this planet as the United States, or the US."

"Excellent, Nybo. I shall pass this information on to the Ministry of Voyaging. What a discovery. Anything else?" asks Albie III.

"Yes, they're very obsessed with ice," replies Nybo.

"Ice! Ice would melt faster than a polar ice cap in that heat," states Albie III.

Nybo responds, "That's what I said, but they insist it can be found behind rocks or trees."

"Hmm," responds Albie III.

Nybo continues. "They're also looking for Anyone! But every time I try to bring up the subject, they start obsessing over ice again."

Suddenly, a meteorite flies by on its way to Earth, and communication is lost due to interference.

After resting for only two hours, the group is up and ready to go. They tell Nybo that traveling must be done when temperatures are at their coolest. They are physically exhausted and move slowly. Many are experiencing cramps from dehydration. "All this debris is a good sign," says Miguel. "We are headed in the right direction."

A young boy named Jose walks with Nybo. Jose tells Nybo that he is from Guatemala. He tells Nybo that there is no law there, no consequences for drugs or rape or murder. He tells Nybo both his father and older brother were murdered, and his mother and sister went out to find food and never returned. Gangs were trying to force him to join with threats of death. He fled on his own and has been walking ever since.

Nybo smiles and nods.

Although the group is moving slowly, some are having a difficult time keeping up. There is a tree not far from them, so they sit in the shade and take a break from the heat of the rising sun. Miguel opens a black gallon jug with about a quart of water in it and hands it to Jose, who takes a small sip. He then hands the jug to the others, who also take small sips. The jug is handed to Nybo with very little water left in it. Nybo does not drink it. He is being cautious of germs from planets he has never heard of before. As Nybo passes the jug to Miguel, he asks, "Why is the jug black?"

"So the sunlight doesn't reflect off of it and attract ICE," answers Miguel. Miguel takes the last sip and tosses the jug onto the ground. Nybo looks behind the tree and shrugs his shoulders.

As the group starts out again, Miguel asks, "Are you scared, Nyboa?"

Nybo tells him, "I'm a little scared and a little excited."

Miguel says, "There are plenty of things to fear in the desert. They all want to kill you. You're lucky you found us. There are lots of stories of strange, unexplainable things—tales about giant snakes, Sasquatch, and UFOs. There are some good tales also, tales about cities made of gold waiting to be discovered. The people who try either die or go loco from the haunting nightmares they're cursed with for the rest of their lives.

"We need to get somewhere soon. We are down to one gallon of water. That's not even enough for one person. In this heat you need about two gallons a day. We are already badly dehydrated. Things are going to get worse very soon."

Just as Miguel begins to ask Nybo how he is in such good shape without any water, they come to a two-track road. There are tire tracks on it.

"We must be getting closer to civilization," says Miguel to the group. The group is very encouraged. Maria starts to cry from joy, but there are no tears due to the dehydration.

They follow the road to the west. The terrain begins to change as the road winds around mesas, large rocks, and cactuses. As they circle a mesa, three wild mustangs are spooked and run full speed away.

"We sure could use some tame ones, eh, amigo. Horses. First, you ride them. Then you eat them," says Miguel. "No telling what's in your taco."

Miguel once had a horse that was stolen and believed to be sold to a meat-packing plant. Nybo is aware of horses from Lone Ranger signals he received. He has never seen one. He thought they were all silver.

"Hiyo, Silver, away," Nybo says, quoting the end of the show.

The group has been walking down the road for two hours. The sun is rising higher in the sky, and the temperature is soaring. Some members of the group are becoming disoriented, walking almost like zombies.

Miguel says, "We can no longer conserve water. People are going to start dying."

They find a shady spot to sit and rest. The final jug passed around by the group and thrown on the ground. Empty. "I hope we find civilization soon," says Miguel.

They will not have to. Civilization has found them. They had been spotted by an ICE drone shortly before their break. An SUV vehicle and a passenger van with no windows suddenly appear. The words *Immigration and Customs Enforcement* are written on them.

CHAPTER 4

ICE AND STONE

The ICE agents approach. The group members are too exhausted and dehydrated to run. They feel more saved than sorry. They are relieved to be found and thankful they will no longer have to endure the unrelenting heat and hardships of crossing the desert.

The agents ask everyone where they claim residency. Mexico, Guatemala, and El Salvador are the answers. Nybo proudly tells them, "Deltoiga."

One of the agents says, "We are asking about countries not towns, pepper pooper."

The agents ask everyone for documentation. The others present papers and cards. Nybo, thinking of his voyager school diploma, says, "I left mine at home."

They are loaded into the van. As Nybo enters, he says, "I have come to talk to you about Anyone."

One of the agents responds, "You can tell them at the field office." The van door slides closed.

They are each given a red plastic cup filled with water from a thermal water jug. Nybo takes a small sip and can hardly swallow. It tastes horrible to him, almost polluted. A much purer version of water is consumed on Deltoiga. This water tastes salty and has so many solids that it is barely drinkable.

Nybo thinks, *Nice place to visit but don't drink the water.*

The van has no windows other than the ones in the driver's cab. There is a steel cage separating the driver's cab from the passengers. It is air-conditioned, and Nybo experiences goose bumps for the first time. Looking at the bumps on his arms, he wonders if they are a reaction to the water.

The ride is rough and bumpy. After a half hour, the van stops, and the driver steps out. The passengers in the van cannot see anything and are wondering what is happening. Ten minutes later, the door slides open, and three more aliens get in.

As the ride resumes, the passengers are mumbling the names and addresses of relatives. Some are actual relatives, and others are names that were provided by the coyote.

One of the new aliens sitting next to Nybo says, "Hey, amigo, you should be practicing your relative's names and addresses so you can recite them naturally during your interview. You look familiar. Have you been detained before?"

Nybo smiles.

"Hey, when they ask you about jobs, tell them you want to be an actor."

The van stops at an ICE field office. While the van is unloading, Nybo notices a woman with a red and swollen arm that has a long, loosely stitched cut on it. He asks the woman what happened to her arm. She responds, "Three men tried to rape me and my eleven-year-old daughter. I was able to fight them off but was cut with a knife during the struggle. I went to a hospital in Mexico where they only gave me drugs. I was there for nine days and received no treatment, only drugs. After the second day, I didn't see my daughter again. As my arm got worse, I was told I needed an operation, but all they did was change my prescription. I left and came to the US to get caught so I could get medical attention. I'm afraid I'm going to lose my arm."

"But it's right there," Nybo says while pointing at her arm.

She gives Nybo a dirty look and tells him, "If they ask you your occupation, tell them you are a coyote."

They walk single file into a crowded room with four unlabeled doors. There are no windows in the room or on the doors. They are each given a numbered ticket and told to wait for their number to be called.

There are no empty seats. People are sitting on the floor and leaning against any available wall space. Others are standing. Nybo hears someone say they have been waiting for over two hours.

He overhears a woman telling someone that she was offered a boat ride across the river. When the boat reached the other side, some men were waiting, and she was kidnapped. She was able to escape after being held two weeks in a semi-truck trailer.

A man standing near Nybo says, "Hey, you look familiar." He tells Nybo this is his third interview in two years. One of the doors opens, and an ICE agent calls out a number. A young child is taken from a woman and brought into the room. The woman is told she will be brought in shortly.

The man tells Nybo, "This is where they start separating everyone. Men are separated from women, husbands from wives, children from their parents. That woman won't see her child again."

A different door opens, and Nybo's number is called. The man says, "That's you, amigo. Hey, that's where I've seen you, on TV."

Nybo enters the room and the door closes.

A generously plump immigration officer sits behind a desk with a computer in front of him. There is a name plate that says John Smith. He points at a chair and says, "Sit." Nybo sits and decides that USAites are very busy people.

John Smith begins asking questions. "Name?"

Nybo responds, "Nybo of Deltoiga. I'm an alien."

John Smith mumbles as he types, "Nyboa Deltoiga. Where you from?"

Nybo looks puzzled as he had just told John Smith. He answers, "Deltoiga."

John Smith deducts that Deltoiga must be a town in Mexico named after the Deltoiga family. He again mumbles while he types, "Mexico," then asks, "Is Deltoiga in southern Mexico?"

Nybo replies, "Oh no. It's much higher up."

John Smith asks, "Is it near the ocean?"

There is a planet near Deltoiga called Theosion and another right next to it called Degulf. The people there are very nice. Nybo is surprised that John Smith knows about Theosion. He replies, "Yes, it is. Right by Degulf. A very nice place."

John Smith states, "Might be worth looking into for my next vacation."

Nybo smiles while saying, "That would be wonderful. Tell them I sent you. They will be very excited."

John Smith gets back to business and asks, "Any relatives in the United States?"

Nybo responds, "I'm not sure. I have a cousin Ef from Deltoiga. He hasn't been heard from for sixteen years."

John Smith again mumbles while he types, "Ephraim Deltoiga. Anybody else?"

Nybo replies, "Well, maybe Jous of Deltoiga."

John Smith mumbles, "Joseph Deltoiga," then asks, "Is that it?"

Nybo states, "Jawshue of Deltoiga. He hasn't been heard from in twelve years."

John Smith mumbles, "Joshua Deltoiga," and then says, "We'll see if we can contact them."

Nybo feels encouraged and states, "Oh! That is wonderful. Thank you, thank you."

John Smith asks, "Employment?"

Nybo asks," What?"

John Smith looks up from the computer and asks, "What do you want to do for work?"

Nybo replies, "I want to be an actor."

With a surprised look, John Smith says, "Seriously? With that face and body. Good luck. Don't quit your day job." He then asks, "What were your past occupations?"

Nybo remembering what the woman with the swollen arm had told him says, "I'm a coyote."

John Smith's attitude changes, and he says, "No bond for you. You will be held until Judge Stone can see you. Here is your alien registration number."

Nybo says, "I came to talk to you about Anyone."

John Smith says, "Tell it to Judge Stone."

Another officer enters and escorts Nybo out of the room. Nybo thanks John Smith again.

The officer takes Nybo down a long hallway and out of a door into a small yard fenced in with razor wire on top. They enter another building. The officer says, "Judge Stone. Man, he's going to eat you alive."

After passing several other doors the officer stops and unlocks one. "You are bed thirty-eight," he tells Nybo. "That's how you will be referred to from now on. You hear someone say thirty-eight, you say, 'Yes, sir,' and come running."

Nybo enters the room and finds bed thirty-eight. The room is very crowded. People are pacing back and forth between the rows of beds. There's barely enough space to walk around.

Nybo is very tired. He takes off his gravity shoes, sets them to full strength, and puts them on the floor next to his bed. He falls asleep almost immediately. It does not take long for his shoes to get noticed. A man walks by and smoothly slips his feet into Nybo's shoes with the intention of walking away in them. He attempts to take the first step, but the gravitational pull is so strong that he cannot move them. He trips and falls face first. He gets up and walks away holding his nose.

It is late when Nybo awakens. Most of the other aliens are sleeping. There's heavy breathing and occasional snoring. Nybo suddenly realizes this is the quietest moment he has experienced since meeting the group in the desert. The verbal communication and external stimulation have been overwhelming. He is mentally taxed but feels this may be his best opportunity to contact Albie III.

He finds he is unable to contact Albie III because of the stress. To relax, he thinks about a game played on Deltoiga called *noggincrackin*. Nybo played the game as a youth. It is the planetary pastime on Deltoiga.

Noggincrackin is a cross between football and ultimate Frisbee. Each player wears a helmet with a hollow, soft rubber pole on top. A round ring called a buzz ring is thrown to a teammate, who catches it with the pole. The defense tries to intercept with their pole. When the ring is caught, the player runs until he is tackled, pushed out of bounds, or scores a digit, a point. There is a professional noggincrackin league with several teams from Deltoiga. When Nybo was a youth, he had dreamed of becoming a professional noggincrackin player, but he could not keep his head in the game.

There is a planet called Pelo where the inhabitants grow hair. Their professional noggincrackin players do not wear helmets. They grow a top knot and braid it to the twelve-inch pole limit. It is very intimidating.

Nybo begins to relax and is finally successful at contacting Albie III. Nybo begins, "Hello, Albie III."

Albie III responds, "Nybo, I was hoping to hear from you. How is the United States?"

Nybo replies, "I met my first USAite today. A nice man called John Smith. He's going to try and find Ef, Jous, and Jawshue."

Albie III is thrilled and says, "That's wonderful, Nybo, excellent."

Nybo continues. "Yes, and he's sending me to one of their leaders to talk about Anyone. A man named Judge Stone."

Albie III can't believe it and states, "Nybo, I have to admit that you are doing an amazing job of making this mission a success. And so quickly."

Nybo feels proud as he answers, "Thank you. Oh, I almost forgot. John Smith is thinking about coming to Deltoiga for a vacation."

Albie III exclaims, "That would be amazing. Tell him he can stay with me and my family."

Nybo smiles and says, "I'll tell him when I see him again. He'll be surprised."

Albie III informs Nybo, "You're becoming a planetary hero, Nybo. Tomorrow the planet is flying the flag at full staff in your honor."

The flag is always flown at half-staff on Deltoiga. It is flown at full staff to honor someone. Nybo blushes as he states, "I don't know if I deserve all that. I'm hon—" A loud sneeze and cough from someone in the room scares Nybo, and communication is lost.

As morning approaches, the other aliens begin to awaken. Nybo talks to some of them who are in beds near his. They are either waiting to see a judge or waiting for a relative to post bond. Nybo learns that some are from other planets called Nicaragua and Honduras. Many have been separated from their families.

A narrow covering on the door slides open, and bed numbers are called out. As each number is called the alien goes to the door and receives a tray with a bowl of mushy oatmeal, a slice of toast with a packet of strawberry jam, an orange, a small carton of juice, and a cup of coffee.

Number thirty-eight is called. Nybo receives a tray and returns to his bed. He sits on the bed and eats for the first time since leaving his spacecraft. He takes a bite of the toast, which is dry. Nybo has a hard time swallowing it. Observing others spreading the jam on their toast, he awkwardly does the same. He takes another bite and finds it is a big improvement. Receiving a sudden, positive sensation from his taste buds, he realizes that strawberry jam is the blue-ribbon food of the multiverse. *They should bottle it and sell it*, he thinks.

Nybo sees the others jabbing a straw into their juice cartons. He does the same and takes a sip of cranberry juice. Throwing his head back with puckered lips and wide eyes, he swallows it, then forcefully exhales with a *paaah* while squinting his eyes and shaking his head.

Tasting the oatmeal, he cannot decide if he likes it. He eats it all. While eating it, he looks at the orange and thinks how nice it is to have a ball to play with. He takes a drink of the coffee and bingo! This is the best liquid ever. He quickly drinks down the coffee. *This is what I'll drink from now on*, he says to himself.

Picking up the ball, he tries to bounce it off the ground. The orange hits the ground with a splat sound and rolls a short distance. "Hey, amigo. What are you doing?" says the alien on the bed across from him. "If you don't want your orange, give it here. I see you like coffee. From now on, you give me your fruit, and I give you my coffee." He hands Nybo his coffee. It is gone in one rapid gulp.

Throughout the day, a window on the door slides open, and a bed number is called. The alien from that bed leaves the room with an officer and never returns. Later in the day, a new alien arrives and takes the bed.

Aliens are walking around the room and pacing back and forth. There are three things to do in the room: walk, think, and sleep.

Nybo is hoping to hear good news about the Deltoigan voyagers John Smith is looking for.

He starts thinking about when he was a tyke and his parents gave him a trisaucer for a gift. He loved it and rode it every day. One day while zipping up and down the driveway, he was flying it too fast and lost control. The trisaucer went through the hedge separating his yard from the Edelsons. A saucer-shaped hole was left in the hedge, but that was not the bad part. The trisaucer skidded through Mrs. Edelson's flower garden, leaving a path of destroyed night lilies, which are extremely difficult to grow. It came to rest in the middle of Mr. Edelson's vegetable garden. No one would believe him that it was an accident. He was grounded for a month and had to mow the Edelsons' lawn for the whole summer. The trisaucer was taken away, and he never saw it again.

Lunch and dinner meals are served. Nybo trades away parts of his meals for tomorrow morning's coffee and jam. Near the end of the day, the window on the door slides open, and number thirty-eight is called. Nybo goes to the door and is told he will see Judge Stone in the morning. Nybo is excited to finally get an opportunity to speak to a leader about Anyone.

"If you want a counselor, let someone know," says the officer.

Nybo contacts Albie III, who agrees to be his counselor. Nybo later informs another officer, "I'll not need counsel tomorrow."

The officer says, "Okay, but Judge Stone is going to eat you alive."

Nybo hears the officer but does not comprehend what he said. He is to excited about the opportunity to talk about Anyone.

When morning arrives, breakfast is delivered. Nybo trades most of his away for coffee and jam. He keeps the greasy hash browns, spreads jam on them, and gobbles them down. The coffee and jam from yesterday's meal trades begin to arrive. Soon, there are over a dozen cups of coffee lined up in front of him. He dips his fingers into the jam and places them into his mouth. He begins drinking coffee. After finishing all the coffees, the alien in the bed across from him says, "That's got to be some kind of record."

Others in the room notice as well. They give Nybo their coffees, chanting, "Go! Go! Go!" as Nybo gulps them down. While drinking his seventeenth cup of coffee, the window on the door slides open, and number thirty-eight is called. Nybo leaves the room with the officer.

While walking to another room in the building that is used for court, Nybo contacts Albie III and informs him it is time to see Judge Stone. The connection is a little fuzzy as the caffeine begins to kick in. The officer says, "You going in there without counsel? Judge Stone is going to eat you alive."

Two things happen simultaneously. The full effects of the caffeine from seventeen cups of coffee hits, and Nybo puts two and two together. With panic, he now understands what is going on. *They want aliens to come to the United States so they can eat them! That's why nobody ever returns to the room after being called! That's what all the officers have been telling me! I'm going to get eaten!*

Nybo enters the room with his heart in his throat and a blank stare in his eyes. He feels weak and empty inside. He is shaking from both fear and caffeine. He stands before the judge who says, "Mr. Deltoiga, you stated that you are both an alien and a coyote. How do you plea?"

Nybo drops to his knees, cups his hands in front of him, and says, "Please don't eat me! Please don't eat me!"

The judge states very firmly while pointing at a chair, "Mr. Deltoiga, sit in that chair. Sit." Nybo sits.

The trial begins. Judge Stone states, "Mr. Deltoiga, this is a very serious matter. I suggest you have counsel present."

Nybo replies, "I do."

Judge Stone looks confused as he says, "You do? Where is he?"

Nybo responds, "He's in my head, sending me messages from Deltoiga."

Judge Stone becomes angered and points his finger at Nybo while stating, "Mr. Deltoiga, I won't allow you to ridicule this court."

The caffeine is at full effect, and Nybo fidgets in the chair. Judge Stone is becoming impatient, and says, "Mr. Deltoiga, would you please sit still?"

Nybo responds rapidly, "I can't. I can't. I can't."

Albie III tunes in and asks, "You can't what?"

Nybo responds, "What?"

Judge Stone asks, "What?"

Albie III then asks, "What?"

As Nybo interprets what Judge Stone is saying, Albie III picks up on his thoughts. When Nybo telepathically sends Albie III a message, he also verbalizes it, creating confusion.

Judge Stone shakes his head and proceeds by saying, "Mr. Deltoiga, it says here you wish to be an actor."

Albie III asks, "An actor?"

Nybo responds, "I'll explain later."

Judge Sone asks, "Explain what later?"

Nybo asks, "What?"

Judge Stone states, "You said you would explain it later."

Nybo says, "I did?"

Judge Stone orders, "Explain it now!"

Nybo tells him, "I want to be a TV actor."

Judge Stone laughs and says, "Mr. Deltoiga, that is a lofty aspiration. Let's face reality. With your looks and body, there's no way possible you could be a TV actor. Perhaps you should consider a career in construction or janitorial services. *For God's sake, would you sit still?*"

Nybo is sitting with his head tilted to the right and positioned upward. His eyes are looking up. Albie III says, "Ask him if he has heard anything about the voyagers."

Nybo says, "Okay, I'll ask."

Judge Stone says, "Ask what?"

Nybo responds, "What?"

The now confused Albie III asks, "What?"

Judge Stone asks, "Did you say you would ask?"

Nybo answers, "Ask what?"

Albie III reminds him, "About the others! Concentrate, Nybo!"

Nybo asks Judge Sone, "Have you heard anything about the other Deltoigans that John Smith is looking for?"

Judge Stone asks, "Who?"

Nybo says, "What?"

Judge Stone now understands the question and says, "Oh yes, about your list of relatives."

Albie III asks, "Who?"

Nybo replies, "It's a long story."

Judge Stone is now irritated and says, "Mr. Deltoiga, I suggest you concentrate on this discussion."

Nybo replies, "That's what Albie III said."

Judge Stone struggles to remain calm and says, "Who? Oh, the counsel in your head. Mr. Deltoiga, there were no Deltoigas found in our system."

Nybo's heart sinks before he states, "Tell John Smith thank you for trying, and if he goes to Deltoiga for his vacation, he can stay with Albie III and his family."

Judge Stone asks, "Who? What?"

Nybo asks, "What?"

Judge Stone can't take anymore and firmly states, "Mr. Deltoiga! For the last time, *sit still!* When you entered this courtroom, there were two options available to me. Now you have given me a third. The first option, which I was ninety percent sure would not happen, was that I could have you deported. The second option, which I was ninety percent sure would happen, was that I could send you to a federal penitentiary. The third option you have now given me, which I'm one hundred percent going to do, is to have you committed to the state hospital in Phoenix for psychiatric evaluation by

Dr. Colgate. He can keep you there for up to three months if he feels it's necessary. You will return to this court after he has made his final analysis."

Albie III suggests, "Tell him about Anyone."

Nybo replies, "Okay."

Judge Stone looks at Nybo and says, "I'm glad you agree."

Nybo asks, "About what?"

Judge Stone asks, "What?"

Albie III says, "What? Concentrate, Nybo."

Nybo says to Judge Stone, "I have come to talk to you about Anyone."

Judge Stone is now totally over this case and says, "You can tell Dr. Colgate about anyone you want. Next!"

Nybo asks, "What?"

Albie III asks, "What?"

An officer leads Nybo out of the courtroom.

CHAPTER 5

JOE KNOWS

Nybo is placed in the rear seat of a patrol car. The driver gets in and says, "You aliens come here and use up all our resources. You guys are trying to turn this place into a socialist society—socialism and crime, the same thing. Both are a redistribution of wealth." The ride remains quiet until they pass a Starbuck's billboard. There is an animal on Deltoiga called a star buck.

Nybo says, "Star bucks, they're all over Deltoiga."

The driver replies, "They're everywhere, Mexico, on the moon. Imagine Starbucks on the moon. Great coffee, no atmosphere."

Nybo thinks that maybe these planets are not so different from each other.

As they drive through Phoenix, Nybo notices a nativity scene in front of a church and asks, "Who are those people?"

The driver isn't sure if Nybo is serious and asks, "Really? What planet are you from?"

"Deltoiga," responds Nybo.

The driver laughs.

Nybo then sees a Christmas tree and says, "Trees that glow. How wonderful. What kind of tree is that?"

The driver is now sure that Nybo is totally nuts and says, "That explains our destination. It's a Christmas tree idiot."

Nybo asks, "Do the glowing seeds fall off of the tree?"

The driver shakes his head, rolls his eyes, and then says, "They're bulbs."

Nybo thinks he must bring some Christmas tree bulbs back to Deltoiga and try to grow some. Deltoigans would love them. Nybo asks, "Are they difficult to grow?"

The driver becomes sarcastic and answers, "Who do I look like, Farmer Brown?"

Nybo responds, "I don't know."

Driving a few more blocks, they pass a Catholic church with a large cross on top. There is an image of Jesus hanging on it. Nybo inquires, "Who is that, and what did he do?"

The driver in disbelief says, "Wow, seriously? That's Jesus Christ. He was hung on the cross because of sin."

Nybo asks, "Sin?"

The driver replies, "Yeah, you know, bad things."

Nybo realizes how lucky he was to have grown up on Deltoiga. If he had grown up here, that could be him instead of Jesus Christ. Nybo says, "The people here must be very well behaved."

The driver is half distracted searching for street names and says, "Yeah, whatever."

They arrive at the hospital. A nine-foot-tall fence made of steel rods surrounds a large, three-story building. The driver pulls up to a gate before pushing a button on a box and speaking to it. The gate swings open. Once they drive through, it swings shut again.

The car stops in front of the building where two large men dressed in white are waiting. The driver gets out of the car and hands one of them a paper to sign. He then says, "Here's your nut job. Good luck."

One of the caregivers replies, "This isn't a clam bake. He'll be undergoing a personality change soon." They laugh.

Nybo says goodbye to the driver, who asks, "Your parents have any kids that lived?"

Nybo responds, "I don't know. I'll ask."

Nybo is escorted into the building and taken to a room where a woman is waiting. She goes over the required forms and asks Nybo if he is taking any medications or has any allergies or any dietary concerns.

"Coffee," says Nybo.

He is told that coffee consumption depends on which medications are prescribed, and then taken to a small room where he is told he will be staying until Dr. Colgate can do an initial assessment. Then he will be placed accordingly. He is given a tour of the facility and yard.

Nybo returns to his room, where he is alone for the first time since meeting the others in the desert. After a short rest, he contacts Albie III, who enthusiastically says, "Nybo! How are things?"

Nybo tells him, "Not bad. Judge Stone has sent me to another leader to talk about Anyone. A man named Dr. Colgate."

Albie III says, "Odd man, that Judge Stone. Keep up the good work, Nybo. You can't believe how famous you've become back here on Deltoiga. They're going to observe a moment of talking in your honor before the noggincrackin game tonight."

Nybo is too tired to feel pride or excitement and responds, "Thank you, thank you. I learned a lot today. There are star bucks on this planet, on Mexico, and the moon."

Albie III interrupts, "Maybe our planets aren't so different."

Nybo continues. "They have amazing trees called Christmas trees. They glow! I'll attempt to bring back some bulbs to plant."

Albie III says, "Deltoigans would love them. Are they difficult to grow?"

Nybo replies, "Who do I look like, Farmer Brown?"

Albie III asks, "What?"

Nybo explains, "I don't know. That's what I was told when I asked."

"Oh," says Albie III.

Nybo tells Albie III, "There was a man called Jesus Christ who was hung on a cross for doing bad things. They put an image of it on top of a building to remind people what will happen if they're bad."

Albie III immediately replies, "They must be very well behaved there. Lucky for you that you grew up on Deltoiga, or that could have been you."

Nybo agrees, stating, "Boy, I'll say. Actually, I did say it. And they—"

A knock on the door breaks Nybo's concentration, and communication is lost.

Nybo is told through the door that it is time for his physical exam. He is taken to Health Services where he waits to be seen. There is another patient waiting who has lost both of his feet to diabetes. He introduces himself as Speedy and says, "You look familiar. I know you from somewhere. You been committed anyplace else?"

Nybo answers, "I was committed to Nock for three weeks."

Speedy shakes his head and says, "Haven't heard of that one." Deciding to have a little fun with Nybo, Speedy asks, "You here to see Dr. Howard?"

Nybo says, "I guess so. I'm here for a physical exam and blood test."

Speedy kiddingly says, "Good luck. He was supposed to cut off my left foot, but he cut off my right foot by mistake. Then he had to cut off my left foot too."

Nybo's forehead wrinkles as he says, "That's horrible."

Speedy continues. "The only good part is another guy was in the room who wore the same size shoes as me. I sold him my shoes for fifteen bucks. Ha-haaaa-ha."

Nybo is called into the examination room. As he enters, Dr. Howard is on his cell phone, with his back toward Nybo. Nybo hears Dr. Howard say, "Two o'clock tee time open at Bellwood. I'll have to leave right now." He turns and, seeing Nybo, says, "Sorry, but an emergency has come up. We'll have to reschedule." Dr. Howard rushes out of the room.

Nybo sleeps through the night. In the morning, he is given one cup of coffee. The caregiver tells Nybo, "The hospital policy is one cup of coffee per patient per day. This place isn't made of money."

Nybo tries to imagine what a place made from money would look like. He is sure he has not seen one yet. Later in the morning, a knock on the door is followed by someone telling Nybo that Dr. Colgate is ready to see him.

While Nybo is being escorted to Dr. Colgate's meeting room, he hopes this will be his opportunity to talk about Anyone and the missing Deltoigan voyagers. Then maybe he can go home.

Dr. Colgate is standing outside of the meeting room, looking over papers. The caregiver introduces Nybo to the doctor. Without looking up, Dr. Colgate says, "Nice to meet you. Have a seat at the table."

Dr. Colgate enters the room and sits across the table from Nybo, who says, "Four out of five dentist recommend Colgate."

Dr. Colgate replies with a straight face, "And five out of five judges. I've been looking over the court documents. Tell me about the voice in your head."

Nybo answers, "Albie III. He's my advisor."

Dr. Colgate is writing notes while he asks, "Any other voices?"

Nybo replies, "Not since I've come to the United States of America."

Dr. Colgate asks, "Do you have any family members who hear voices?"

Nybo says, "Of course, all of them. Everyone from Deltoiga hears voices."

Dr. Colgate gets a distressed look on his face and says, "Yes, Deltoiga. Tell me about your environment growing up."

Nybo feels happy that someone is interested in his home planet. "Deltoiga is a wonderful place to grow up. It's such a happy place. Although now that I think about it, the Edelsons could get a little grumpy from time to time."

Dr. Colgate asks, "The Edelsons?"

"Our neighbors."

While Nybo tells him about the trisaucer incident, Dr. Colgate looks out of the window and gets distracted by two new female nurses passing by. He writes down *tricycle*.

Nybo tells him, "I hung a dummy from a tree in their yard once."

Dr. Colgate writes, *Possible suicidal tendencies.*

Nybo continues. "I was sent to Nock for three weeks."

While Nybo tells him about flipping the log around the moon, Dr. Colgate realizes that he forgot to make dinner reservations for this evening, and blurts out, "Jesus Christ."

Nybo agrees. "I know. I was lucky not to have grown up here. Look, I really need to talk to you about Anyone."

Dr. Colgate responds, "Anyone mental. Unfortunately, I have a pressing matter that needs my attention right away. I have a pretty good idea of my analysis and recommendations. I need blood work results before I begin your medication program. Dr. Howard has agreed to see you right away." Dr. Colgate leaves the room to make his dinner reservation as Nybo is taken to health services.

Three other patients are waiting to see the doctor. Speedy is just leaving after a diabetic check. He sees Nybo and says, "Nice shoes. You can get twenty bucks for those after Doc gets through with ya. Ha-ha."

One of the other patients introduces himself as Jeff and says, "You look like a reasonable guy. Can I talk to you? Nyboa, right?"

Nybo says, "It's Nybo. Sure, let's talk."

Jeff looks in all directions and then leans close to Nybo. Talking just above a whisper, he says, "Nyboa, I need your help. They got all the outlets bugged. The lights are either cameras or bugs. Why would they do that?"

Nybo, with concern, answers, "I don't know."

Jeff replies, "Shhh. Keep it down. There's more. All the books in the library have been altered. All the dates have been changed by one year."

Nybo asks, "Why?"

Jeff looks around again and says, "It's all a state-run conspiracy. I have got to tell you about my sister. She called here and left me a message to call her. When I did, her phone had been disconnected. Two weeks later, she died. It wasn't just a coincidence. Everyone who checks into this either dies or disappears. Sheriff Colby, Judge Markham, all gone. My lawyer's in on it with them. He can't be trusted. Can you help me out Nyboa?"

Nybo gets called into the office and leaves Jeff without answering. Dr. Howard greets him and asks, "So Nyboa, any health concerns?"

Nybo replies, "I'm a little concerned about the bugs in the outlets."

Dr. Howard says, "Really? We just had this place fumigated a little over a month ago. Well, that's what you get with a state-run operation—bugs in the outlets. Let's get you examined. First order of business is to get some blood work done."

A bright flash of lightning occurs simultaneously with a deafening clap of thunder. A heavy rain starts bouncing off the window, hitting so hard it seems it could break the glass. The lights flicker and go out. The building goes on auxiliary power. An announcement is made for all patients to return to their rooms. Dr. Howard says, "Well, there's eighteen holes that won't get played. We'll have to take a rain check, sport. Off you go now."

Nybo asks, "Direct deposit?"

Dr. Howard says, "What? Oh, very funny."

Nybo once heard a public service announcement about direct deposit of tax refund checks being faster.

Nybo is told he will be moved after the storm. As he is escorted back to his room, another caregiver approaches and says to the escort, "He'll be moving to room 218."

The escort replies, "They're putting him in with space cadet Joe? How about you take him?"

The other caregiver says, "No way. I've heard enough about dimensions and aliens. Once Joe gets going, you can never get away." He looks at Nybo and says, "I hope you brought your earplugs."

The storm is severe but short. Nybo is taken to a different area of the hospital where the movement is less restricted. He is to be placed with another patient so they can keep an eye on each other in case of suicidal ideation.

Arriving at room 218, the caregiver knocks on the door and then quickly opens it. The new roommate, Joe, is standing near a window, wearing an Area 51 T-shirt. Joe is of medium height and stature. He has short, dark-brown hair and a pointed nose that's slightly longer than average. Joe is a self-proclaimed expert on aliens.

Joe looks at the caregiver and immediately begins talking. "All these psychiatrists and psychologists think they know so much. They need to start thinking outside the box. Earth is about to enter the fourth dimension. Then they'll find out how little they know."

The caregiver introduces Nybo.

Joe continues. "NASA scientists too, they don't know anything. They still think the sun is hot!"

The caregiver replies, "I believe you're right, Joe. They do think the sun is hot. I got to run. Bye."

Joe says, "Wait, let me tell you about the Grays. The more you know the better you can protect yourself from abduction."

The caregiver replies, "You have told me about the Grays. Like ten times now. Tell it to Nyboa." He turns and exits.

Joe turns toward Nybo and asks, "You ever met an alien from outer space?"

Nybo says, "Of course."

Joe says, "You bet you have. They disguise themselves as humans. They're everywhere. Some even have jobs: Walmart, McDonald's."

Nybo realizes that Joe seems knowledgeable about aliens and asks, "Have you ever heard of Ef, Jous, or Jawshue?"

Joe quickly responds, "No," and continues. "The Grays can no longer reproduce in their environment, so they have come here to reproduce with humans. It's the only way they can survive."

Nybo asks, "The Grays?"

Joe explains, "Yeah, they're highly intelligent. They abduct humans, cows, anything they think might help them. They've learned to clone sheep. They've already been cloning themselves. It's all very secret. They hide it from the government. I try to explain it to the doctors and caregivers, but nobody will listen to me. Do you believe in space travel?"

Nybo replies, "Yes, that's how I got here."

Joe pauses then says, "Right. The Grays have Elvis too."

Nybo excitedly says, "Alphous II. I know him!" Alphous II was the sanitation engineer at the voyager school on Deltoiga.

Joe isn't sure if Nybo is mocking him and says, "You're more nuts than I am. Do you think you're a Gray?"

Nybo replies, "No, I'm a Deltoigan."

Joe asks, "What do they look like?"

Nybo briefly changes into his natural Deltoigan form and then back to his Danny Devito–looking human form. Joe gasps for air as he loses all the color from his face. He steps back, placing his hand over his heart. His mouth is wide open, along with his eyes. He is frozen and cannot speak because of fright. Moments pass and Joe still cannot form words.

Nybo explains about the missing Deltoigan voyagers and the messages about Anyone.

Joe is finally able to move. He runs to the door, throws it open, and begins yelling in a panic, "He's an alien! He's an alien!"

Caregivers come rushing into the hallway. Joe continues to scream, "He's an alien. A real alien! Not a Gray. An alien!"

The caregivers are all aware that Nybo is being detained by ICE and reassuringly say, "We know, Joe. We know. It's okay. It's okay. We know.

Joe says, "You do? He's not a Gray. He's like Deltoyma or something."

The caregivers again reassuringly say, "We know, Joe. It's okay. He's from Deltoiga. Do you know of any Grays coming from there?"

Joe, both scared and confused, replies, "No. Is it really okay? You know he's from Deltoiga?"

A caregiver places his hands upon Joe's shoulders and says, "Everything is just fine, Joe." The caregiver turns to Nybo and says, "Tell him everything's fine."

Nybo replies, "I'm just here to talk to you about Anyone."

The caregiver laughs and says, "Just don't talk about me. See, Joe? Everything is all right. You guys can talk about anyone."

Joe spends the rest of the day inquiring about space travel and star systems. Nybo tells Joe about John Smith, how he tried finding Ef, Jous, and Jawshue, and how Judge Stone said they were not in this star system.

Nybo tells Joe, "I'm waiting to talk to Dr. Colgate about the United States of America voyager they're looking for. Then I can go home."

Joe says, "I suppose you're going to abduct me."

Nybo answers, "No."

Joe is disappointed and says, "Oh. Well, can I just go with you?"

Nybo states, "It would be an awfully tight fit in the spacecraft."

Joe, almost begging, says, "I'm a light packer."

Nybo continues. "Besides, it would have to be approved by the Wisdom Core. I don't know if they would go for it."

Joe becomes confused as they are called to dinner.

After dinner, Joe and Nybo go to the commons room to watch television. Nybo is aware of television but has never watched one. *Wheel of Fortune* is just beginning. The contestants introduce themselves.

Contestant #1 is a medium-build, energetic, well-dressed man who says, "Hi, I'm William Plug from Miami. My friends call me Sparky."

The host replies, "Sparky, because of your last name?"

Contestant #1 says, "Uh, I never thought about it.

Contestant #2 is a short, small man with narrow, rounded shoulders. He has a bushy black beard and long black hair. He introduces himself. "Hi, my name is Eric Bush, and I'm from Cleveland, Ohio. They call me Woofy."

The host says, "Perhaps because you look like Eddie's doll on *The Munsters?*"

Contestant #2 says, "Uh, I never thought about it."

Contestant #3 is a three-hundred-pound black woman who says, "Hi, I'm Pamuhl of Deltoiga. I reside in Hollywood. They call me Spaghetti Betty."

The host says, "We'll just stick with Pamula."

Nybo's jaw opens so wide his chin practically hits the floor. Sitting almost frozen, he stares at the television. Joe notices and asks, "What's the matter?"

Nybo is in shock as he answers, "That's Pamuhl, the other missing voyager."

CHAPTER 6

THE STORY OF PAMUHL

It was two and a half weeks until the new millennium. The Edelsons were hosting an early celebration this evening—not only for the new millennium but also for Mrs. Edelson's sister, Pamuhl, who would be embarking on an incredible space journey the day after tomorrow. The magazine *Better Planet and Garden* was going to be there. The magazine would not only be covering a story on Pamuhl but also featuring Mrs. Edelson's night lily garden on the cover. It was the toast of the planet.

Just hours before the celebration was to begin, little Nybo was riding his trisaucer up and down the driveway when next thing he knew he was in the Edelsons' yard, parked in the middle of Mr. Edelson's vegetable garden. Mrs. Edelson's night lily garden was ruined. Of course, it was the talk of the party.

Everyone attending the party congratulated Pamuhl. Although it wasn't planned, Pamuhl thought a little speech. Everyone at the party consoled Mrs. Edelson. Although it was planned, Mrs. Edelson did not think a speech. A lot of ill thinking toward Nybo was being done, thoughts like, *If that were my kid, I'd teach him some respect*, and *Nock is knocking*.

The worst thought someone projected was, *That boy will freeze in Chell.*

Someone else agreed. *Yes, that boy will be another drop of water on the glacier.*

You mean bucket of water, someone added.

Deltoigans believe that when you die, you either go to Good Haven or to Chell. Good Haven is their version of heaven. Pure thinking and clean living are your ticket in. "Good behavin' gets you into Good Haven" is the old adage. Chell is their version of hell. In Chell, you freeze rather than burn. Once frozen, they warm you just enough to experience the agony of thawing. As soon as the pain of thawing begins to subside, they freeze you again. The cycle continues endlessly. It's no way to spend eternal life.

Two weeks later, on Earth there was a celebration on the eve of the new millennium, more of a farewell-to-life-as-we-know-it party. Below the mansion where the party was being held, there was a survival bunker surrounded by bedrooms. The party guests intended to spend the next year or two living there. They believed that when the clock struck midnight, the world would be thrown into chaos, making survival on the planet uncertain.

The emcee made an announcement. "For those of you who did not attend last year's survival party, let me tell you what to expect. At midnight when the power fails, a trail of solar lights will lead you to the bunker entrance. Once inside of the bunker, you will find your name posted on the door of your room. So, for the next two hours, dance, gorge yourselves with fine food, have fun. Life as you have known it is about to end. This is the true millennium, folks, not a phony like last year."

There was disagreement on Earth about when the new millennium would begin, the year 2000 or the year 2001.

One of the partygoers, Woody, was employed as a maintenance man at the mansion. Woody would not be going into the bunker. He wouldd be taking care of the place during the years of chaos if it should happen to survive. Woody's goal was to become an actor. After graduating high school, Woody had gone to Hollywood, hoping to catch a break. He was rejected on every gig he attempted to get.

"Sorry, but with your looks and body, nobody will take you seriously as an actor," he had been told. He returned home, broke and discouraged, but he never gave up on his dream. Woody could pass for the twin brother of Danny Devito.

Working in construction for a year wore him out. Blistered hands and a sore back were not the way to make a living. After a hard day's work, he rarely had the energy to go to the playhouse. When the opportunity to work at the mansion came along, he jumped on it.

There were other mansion employees attending. Except for Cheeves, the chauffer, none were invited into the bunker. It was all about taking care of the mansion.

One of the maids in attendance was working her way through law school. Woody had noticed her several times before. She sat by herself for most of the party. Shortly before midnight, Woody worked up the courage to cross the room and talk to her. "Hi, I'm Woody. I thought you might like someone to talk to."

She responded, "I'm Autumn. Woody sounds like a forest."

He replied, "That's my last name. I'm Woody Forest."

She smiled and said, "Mine is Leaf. I'm Autumn Leaf."

"Sounds like you two were made for each other," said a bystander.

Woody and Autumn hit it off. The emcee announced that it was time for the countdown. "This is it, folks."

Ten, nine, eight, seven, six, five, four, three, two, one— you could hear the last piece of confetti hit the floor as the crowd sat stunned in silence. The lights were still on. After what seemed like an hour of stillness, the emcee broke the silence.

"Oh."

R J R

"Well."

"Huh."

"Well … everyone just go home."

The stunned guests exited the party.

New Year's Eve on Deltoiga went differently. The masses gathered at Hour Circle in the big city of Old Kroy to watch the square go up. The count up begins: one, two, three, four, five, six, seven, eight, nine, ten. But just as the crowd started to collectively think cheering, the power failed. All Chell broke loose. The planet was in total darkness. Land-rovers would not start. Clocks stopped. People were thinking screaming. It was total chaos. The new millennium caught Deltoiga totally unprepared.

It took Deltoiga over a month to return to near normal. All financial records were lost. People were asked to go to their banks and tell them how much money should be in their accounts and how much they owed on their mortgages and land-rover loans. It was three weeks before anybody realized that Pamuhl had not returned from space.

New Year's Eve in space was lonely. Pamuhl thought about home and the celebration she was missing at Old Kroy. She glanced back and forth from the detailed chart she was working on, to what was going on outside of her spacecraft. She frantically worked at the purpose of her voyage, to chart stars and planets previously unknown to Deltoiga. Pamuhl had gone further into space than any previous voyager had ever been.

Being extremely intelligent, Pamuhl had sailed through voyager school with ease, graduating at the top of her class. With writing, mechanical, and mathematical skills far above the others, she was the obvious choice for this mission. Two weeks out from Deltoiga, she was approaching the midpoint of her voyage. In a few days, she would begin the return trip home.

The year was 2000. Nybo was five years old and aware of Pamuhl through news accounts given by the *Daily Deltoigan*. Pamuhl had become a planetary hero.

Communication with her wisdom guide, Albie II, had become sporadic. It had been a day and a half since the last contact, which was interrupted when she flew too close to a comet. Albie II, the father of Albie III, was the son of Albie, one of the voyaging pioneers on Deltoiga. Pamuhl's spacecraft was titled the Albie.

Pamuhl had mixed emotions about reaching the midpoint of the journey. A part of her wanted to press on indefinitely while a part of her wanted to be back on Deltoiga, living in comfort and having other Deltoigans to communicate with. She wondered what life as a hero would be like. She would never know.

It was 0001 hours. The new year began. The date was January first, two thousand and one. The new millennium has arrived, and all the instruments on the spacecraft went haywire. Lights flickered and went out, and sparks flew as the spacecraft violently shook, causing Pamuhl to lose control. The spacecraft spun and flipped in darkness. Pamuhl was frozen in a state of terror, sitting in the dark. Experiencing total confusion for the first time in her life, Pamuhl sat motionless for several minutes.

Wondering if the auxiliary power would work, her hands groped at the control panel, looking for the switch. Unable to find it, she sat back and thought, *So this is how it ends.* After a moment of reflecting on her life, she realized there was nothing to do other than look for the auxiliary power switch. Even if it took the rest of her life.

Moments later, she found the switch. When she flipped it on, nothing happened. *Well, I tried*, she thought. *I guess we Deltoigans aren't as smart as we think.* Slapping the control panel, she felt a different switch. Flipping it on, she has axillary power.

A couple of lights came on. After a few seconds, they went off. They came on again, then went off, then back on, then off. This continued for several minutes. Pamuhl managed to somewhat stabilize the spacecraft and get it headed toward a small, bright planet. Once within the paltry gravitational pull of the planet, she turned the power switch off, hoping there would be enough power left to assist with the emergency landing when the time came.

When the spacecraft was close enough to the planet to begin the landing procedure, she flipped the power switch on. Nothing happened. She desperately flipped the switch on and off several times. Giving up, she sat back in hopelessness. As tears began to form in her eyes, the lights came on. Pamuhl quickly began the landing procedure. The lights went off, back on, back off, back on. The spacecraft was slowed a little, but not enough for a safe landing.

She fought to keep the spacecraft upright as it slammed down on the planet with a tremendous jolt. Pamuhl experienced a slight case of brain rattle adding to the confusion. The spacecraft withstood the impact and remained intact. Pamuhl looked out a window and, in the distance, saw an American flag. She had landed on the moon. The lights went out and stayed out.

CHAPTER 7

TIME TO GO

Nybo sees a caregiver and begins ranting, "I must go to Hollywood. Pamuhl is there! She's the one I have been looking for! I must see her! I must talk to her! I need to get to Hollywood!"

The caregiver responds, "Okay, Nyboa, relax. Relax. We know you want to go to Hollywood. I'm sure Pamula is a very lovely woman. She isn't going anywhere; she'll be there when you get there."

Nybo desperately answers, "I need to go now! I'm going to bring her home!"

The caregiver sternly states, "Dr. Colgate will decide when you can leave."

Nybo, in a panic, says, "I must see him right away!"

The caregiver informs Nybo, "He'll be here in the morning. Maybe you can see him then."

There is no way Nybo can sleep. When he is not tossing and turning in bed, he is pacing back and forth in the room. Joe cannot sleep because of Nybo's restlessness and asks, "You're not going to sleep at all, are you?"

Nybo responds, "I need to see Dr. Colgate in the morning so I can get going."

Joe shakes his head and laughs. "You really don't get it, do you?"

Nybo continues. "This is why I'm here. In the morning, I'll tell Dr. Colgate about Anyone. I'll go to Hollywood and get Pamuhl. Then I can return home."

Joe informs Nybo, "You're not going anywhere. They aren't going to let you leave. To them, you aren't even a person—you're a condition. One that needs fixing. If they can't fix it, they keep experimenting, indefinitely. No, they won't let you leave. They'll just load you up with medications to keep you passive."

Nybo replies, "They have to let me leave. This is the reason I'm here. Medications?"

Joe continues. "You ever notice how the people in here sleep most of the day? That's because of the medications they're given. You see Dr. Colgate and start making a stink about not being able to leave, or start obsessing over Pamula and Hollywood, you won't be pacing around anymore. You'll be living in la-la land like the rest of them, moving like a zombie with a confused look on your face all the time."

Nybo insists, "Dr. Colgate wouldn't do that to me. He's so nice. He said he thought he could help me."

While laughing, Joe states, "With your condition. He can help you with your condition. Dr. Nice Guy is more mental than half of the patients in here. The guy put his dog in a cardboard box for a month because he thought he had a condition. He cut holes for the head, legs, and tail. Look, it's best if you don't see Dr. Colgate tomorrow, but if you do, stay calm. Be real cool and say as little as possible. You have the right to remain silent, and if you don't, they'll make you silent in the long run. I've got an idea that I think will help you. I'll tell you about it later, so you don't accidentally blab it to anybody, especially Dr. Fruitcake. I have a visit with my brother tomorrow afternoon. I'll explain everything after that."

In the morning, Nybo is called to Dr. Colgate's meeting room. Dr. Colgate doesn't greet Nybo and says, "So, Nyboa, the caregivers report that you have been stirring the pot a bit. You got Joe all worked up yesterday afternoon, and then you had an anxiety attack last night. I can give you some medication for that condition. It'll probably help you to sleep also."

Nybo begins thinking that Joe was right. Dr. Colgate continues. "Have you heard any voices in your head since your last visit?"

Nybo realizing that he has not contacted Albie III to tell him about Pamuhl answers, "No."

Dr. Colgate proceeds. "Good. It's safe to say that you are schizophrenic. I can start you on medication to help with that condition. The good news is there are several different fixes we can experiment with. We'll get you fixed up sooner or later. Now the medication may cause confusion, and slow you down a bit, but you'll adjust to it in no time. And if you don't, you'll probably have a psychotic episode. We have medications for that also. Any questions?"

Nybo grumbles, "Argh."

Dr. Colgate checks his watch and states, "Good. Still waiting on blood work. You go directly to health services and see Dr. Howard."

Nybo is determined to leave this place. Following through on his mission, he states, "I need to tell you that we haven't seen or heard from your voyager Anyone."

Dr. Colgate drops his head and shoulders and, with a sigh, says, "I really don't have time for this. I was afraid putting you with Joe was a bad idea. There just aren't a lot of options right now."

Since moving to room 218, Nybo can go to meetings without an escort. He arrives at Health Services and finds other patients waiting to see Dr. Howard. Nybo sits quietly wondering how he will find Pamuhl. The only option he can think of is to wait for a quiet moment and try to telepathically connect with her.

A very large, muscular man is escorted into health services by two caregivers. The man is in restraints, and each caregiver has a hold of one of his arms. There is a high-security area in the hospital where this man resides. They stop at the nurse's station. The man looks at Nybo and, with a snarl, asks, "What are you here for?"

Nybo tells him, "I'm here for blood work."

The nurse points at a room and tells the caregivers they can wait in there. As they walk toward the room, the man looks back at Nybo and says, "Don't worry. I'll give the doc some blood for you."

Nybo continues to sit quietly while thinking, *They can't really be detaining me. I'll cooperate for now so they don't give me medication, but it's time for me to go.*

As Nybo wonders how he will get to Hollywood, his concentration is broken when a man is rushed in with several bleeding cuts on his arms. Nybo notices the man's arms are badly scared. Some of the scars are a foot long. The man often engages in self-injurious behavior.

"He's at it again," yells the caregiver.

The man is taken into a room, and Dr. Howard rushes in. After ten minutes, Dr. Howard exits the room. As Dr. Howard is about to enter the room with the restrained man, he notices Nybo waiting and says, "Oh, there you are. We'll squeeze you in next, scooter. You won't take long. Then Dr. Colgate can get off my back."

Dr. Howard enters the room. After thirty seconds, screaming and loud banging comes from inside. The caregivers call for backup. Dr. Howard rushes out of the room, blood on his face. The restrained man bit his own lip and tongue, making them bleed enough that his mouth had filled with HIV-infected blood. As Dr. Howard leaned in close to the man, the man spit the infected blood into Dr. Howard's mouth and eyes. He then started spitting at the caregivers. Dr. Howard rushes into the bathroom where he spits into the sink and flushes his eyes and mouth with running water.

Hospital security arrives along with additional caregivers. There is an announcement for all patients to return to their rooms. Once again, Nybo leaves health services without a blood test, the results of which would reveal that he is not human.

Nybo sits on his bed while the anxiety continues to build. Unable to sit still, he paces around the room and decides he must leave. Finding a way to Hollywood is a risk he will have to chance. Nybo mutters out loud, "I'm leaving."

As he reaches for the doorknob, the door swings open. Joe enters the room, returning from the visit he had with his brother. Nybo informs him, "I can't wait any longer. I'm leaving."

Joe replies, "Sit down a minute, Nybo. I have a plan; we'll be in Hollywood tomorrow morning."

Joe moves a small dresser from in front of an outlet and begins to remove the outlet cover. Nybo asks, "Does your plan involve bugs?"

Joe responds, "Just watch for staff." After removing the outlet cover, Joe pulls out a plastic bag containing twenty white pills and says, "I've been saving these for a special occasion."

Nybo asks, "What is it?"

"It's enough Haldol to knock out an elephant," replies Joe.

Nybo asks, "What's an elephant, and why would we want to knock one out?"

Joe states, "It's not for an elephant. Here's the plan. The caregivers shift change is at eight thirty tonight. They all go into the meeting room for about ten minutes. Thelma Lou, the camera monitor, is the only one left watching the place. She and the maintenance guy, Larry, are involved in an affair. This is their alone time. Whew, if the cameras were reversed, that would be a show. Anyway, most nights, the cameras go unmonitored during this time. I've checked it out a few times by sneaking around for a couple of minutes. So tonight when the staff are in the meeting room, I sneak into their break room and put the Haldol into their coffee pot. All the caregivers on this wing drink coffee. By ten o'clock, they'll be sleeping, or at least be unable to move. My brother meets us at the north fence at ten thirty, throws a rope over, and, Hollywood, here we come."

Nybo inquires, "Will it work?"

"Just don't forget to grab your shades," Joe replies confidently.

While Joe is explaining the plan, his brother, Moe, visits the local Walmart. Moe has been in and out of prison for petty crimes most of his adult life. He managed to hold down a job for almost a year until he was replaced by a robot. Figuring that with no job he will likely go back to prison, he decided he had better visit Joe, since it would be the last chance for a while. The two brothers are the only family that each other have. So, after receiving his final check, he jumps into his fifteen-year-old white Camaro and heads for Phoenix.

Moe grabs two home-safety fire ladders from off the shelf. Placing them near the exit, he walks through the store. Moe grabs a doughnut and a quart of milk. He eats half of the doughnut and drinks some of the milk. Walking by the checkout, he places them in an unsuspecting woman's cart. As the woman leaves the store, Joe tells the store greeter that he saw the woman take the milk and doughnut without paying for them.

While the greeter chases after the woman, Moe grabs a bag out of the recycle bin, puts the fire ladders in it, and leaves the store. The greeter is looking over the woman's receipt and does not notice Moe walk out. Moe is relieved after successfully completing phase one of his part of the plan. The relief is short-lived as he turns his attention to the escape. He spends the rest of the afternoon impatiently waiting in his hotel room.

Eight thirty-two. The caregivers pile into the meeting room. Joe waits a moment and then opens the door and pokes his head into the hallway. After looking in both directions, he creeps down the hall and uses a laminated Monopoly deed card to unlock the break room door. Walking over to the kitchenette area, he finds the coffee pot sitting on the warming pad with less than a cup left in it. He mumbles to himself, "Those idiots filled their cups before the meeting."

It has been years since Joe has made coffee. After dumping out the pot, Joe fills the coffee maker with water. While doing so, he begins to panic. He thinks, *This was supposed to be a two-second mission. Things aren't going well.* He searches unsuccessfully for filters. After looking through all the cupboards and drawers, he decides the great escape is over.

As he turns to leave, he notices a towel on the countertop. Lifting the towel, he finds a stack of filters. Joe's hands are shaking as he attempts to separate one filter from the others. A second feels like an eternity. Not giving up, Joe finally succeeds and places a filter into the basket.

Grabbing a large spoon, he begins to scoop coffee into the filter. After putting in the seventh scoop, he realizes he has no idea how much to put in. He finds directions on the can but is unable to stop shaking or to concentrate and cannot read them. *That's probably enough*, he decides.

As he attempts to place the can of coffee on the counter, he drops it onto the floor spilling the coffee. With his hand, he shovels some of the coffee back into the can and places the can on the counter. Using the towel that had covered the filters, he sweeps the remaining coffee against the base of the counter.

Joe starts for the door in a panic. Stopping himself, he goes back and pushes the filter into position. He pushes the start button and runs to the door. "I forgot to put in the Haldol," he says to himself. "It's too late. I've got to get out of here."

He manages to calm himself, go back to the kitchenette, and puts the pills into the pot. Upon reaching the door, he slowly opens it and pokes his head into the hallway. All clear. He hurries on tiptoes back to his room. As he enters the room, he looks back to see the doorknob on the meeting room door turning. Quickly closing his door, he leans back against it.

Nybo excitedly asks, "Did you do it? What took you so long? Did you do it?"

Joe pants, his head spinning as he looks at Nybo and says, "I don't know. I don't know. I think so." The two roommates then sit anxiously on their beds.

CHAPTER 8

GRAY AREA

Life on the moon had not gone well. Pamuhl had found it difficult to breathe outside of the spacecraft. The short treks she had taken had been unproductive—no water, no tillable soil, not a single tree or living thing. The United States flag had been the only positive thing. It now covered a window in the spacecraft, keeping out the light, which had been increasing daily. Pamuhl's one peaceful moment came when she used the flagpole to carve a message on the moon's surface. It said, *Pamuhl was here.*

Pamuhl realized that there was no hope for a rescue. Staying with the spacecraft would result in certain death. Any hope of survival lay somewhere out on the planet. Staying with the spacecraft would result in a 100 percent chance of death; roaming the planet was only a 99.99 percent chance of death. Packing what little supplies remained, she would leave the spacecraft behind tomorrow and face the harsh reality of the planet.

Lying down for the last time in the spacecraft, Pamuhl quickly realized that she was not likely to sleep. *I might as well leave now*, she reasoned. *I'll give it an hour, and if I'm not asleep, I'm gone.*

The spacecraft began to shake violently, and Pamuhl reacted by bolting up into a sitting position. Her heart beat wildly as a blinding light encompassed the spacecraft. Shielding her eyes with one hand, she attempted to stand. The shaking did not allow it. The spacecraft began to rise and left the surface of the planet.

The craft was gliding through space at a speed far exceeding its capabilities. Filled with fright and fear, Pamuhl worried if the spacecraft could handle the stress of traveling at this rate of speed. Its integrity had already been compromised when it slammed down onto the planet. If it could not, it meant death. Pamuhl suddenly realized that this was an improvement. Now there was only a 99.98 percent chance of death.

The craft had been speeding through space for three days. There had not been an attempt by her captors to contact her. Unable to see anything outside of the spacecraft because of the unceasing, blinding light, Pamuhl thought about how many stars and planets they must have passed. There would not be enough material on board to chart them. She could barely keep up with the charting while traveling at a normal rate of speed; it would be impossible to chart anything at this speed.

The speed of travel began to steadily decrease, until it came to what seemed like a crawl. It eventually came to a standstill. Pamuhl felt the spacecraft descending. The craft came to a stop with a slight jar. All unsecured items fell to the floor. *Well, at least there's gravity*, she thinks. The blinding light disappeared. Once her eyes had time to adjust, she could see that she was in some type of a container. Another day passed without contact from her captors.

Pamuhl was awakened by a door slamming closed. Looking out a window, she saw five tall aliens in white coats, holding clipboards, standing near her craft. The tallest stood eight feet high; the shortest was just under seven feet tall. Large, brown, oblong eyes sat below a slightly rounded head that tapered down to a pointed chin. A small, slit mouth rested below a defined nose. The whitish-gray head was supported by a long, skinny neck. Pamuhl had been abducted by the Grays.

Communication was done telepathically. Pamuhl learned that she was on the red star called Betelgeuse in the constellation Orion. She was told one of the Grays' pilots had been on his way to Earth to abduct a human when he had noticed her spacecraft on the moon. The pilot had brought her back to Betelgeuse to see if the Grays could somehow assist her. She would find out this was a lie.

Pamuhl was ordered to exit her spacecraft. Her instincts told her not to. *What choice do I have?* she thought. *They haven't killed me yet. Things are getting better. Now there's only a 99.97 percent chance of death.*

She exited the craft and said, "I'm Pamhul of Del—" It was the last thing she would remember for six years.

It was now the year 2007, six years since Pamuhl had been abducted from the moon. She heard a voice for the first time since the brief telepathic communication with her abductors. Her mind was in a fog as she heard someone say, "Welcome back. You must be hungry."

Pamuhl asked, "Where am I? How did I get here? Who are you?"

As her vision began to clear, she heard, "I'm Zeta. We are in Mexico, on the planet Earth. You were held captive for six years by the Grays."

Pamuhl was confused. "The who? The what? The where?"

"It's always confusing waking up from a six-year coma. My name is Zeta. I'm a member of the Black League, the resistance to the Grays. They intend to dominate all planets and all living things. They abducted you for their own purposes, to experiment with you. When they were finished with you, they brainwashed you and dropped you here."

Pamuhl asked, "What kind of experiments? I don't remember any of that."

Zeta explained, "Many generations ago, the king on Betelgeuse was concerned about the population revolting against his family's right to rule. Through mind control, the population was convinced that reproduction was undesirable and irresponsible. After several generations, their reproductive organs no longer functioned due to atrophy."

"What's that got to do with me?"

Zeta replied, "They began cloning themselves but found each new generation of clones were genetically weaker than the previous generation. That is when they began abducting humans, animals, and other aliens to experiment with their genetic makeup. They're looking for a race most compatible for breeding."

As her head began to clear, Pamuhl said, "They sure abducted me all right. They must be very advanced."

"The Grays are highly intelligent, but they lack emotions and compassion. They have found humans to be most compatible, but humans are weak, lazy, and slow-witted. They continue to search for a better race. They're also looking for genetic combinations to create the ultimate warrior to assist them with supreme domination."

Pamuhl stated, "So they just take whoever they want?

Zeta told her, "The Grays threatened to destroy Earth in 1954. Then President Eisenhower made a deal with them. The Grays were granted permission to abduct humans without interference in exchange for technological secrets. That's where the military got stealth technology for bombers and planes. Stem cell research, the Grays. Bermuda triangle, the Grays."

Pamuhl shook her head, then tapped it with one hand. "It's all very confusing. Hey! My shoes, where are my shoes?"

"The Grays took them. We must get going before their Earth organization finds you. There's a safe house near the United States border. We can stay there until you are cleansed."

Without her shoes, Pamuhl had a difficult time with gravity and walking. Zeta told her to take a human form so she would not be easily noticed. A Weight Watchers flyer being blown by the wind tumbled along the ground and paused in front of them. There was a picture of a large woman on it. To compensate for the lack of gravity, Pamuhl decided to resemble the picture and became a three-hundred-pound black woman.

It took a month for Pamuhl's mind to be cleared of the brainwashing. She retained the English she had been taught by the Grays. Ready to experience life on Earth, Pamuhl would be taken to a safe house on the US side of the border. From there, she would be transported to Los Angles. Hollywood, to be exact.

Zeta said, "I hope you have good luck, Pamuhl. When the transport arrives in Hollywood, you will be met by a member of the Black League. He'll help you to settle into your new home. Makeshift home that is. The Grays will be looking for you. If they find you, they will punish you. Then you will be sent to a work planet to spend the rest of your life performing hard labor. They won't search for you among a bunch of undesirable humans. That's why you will be living in a homeless community. Be careful, Pamuhl. The Grays can be very deceitful."

CHAPTER 9

BI-BI

Ever since the visit, Moe has gone over the plan repeatedly. As time draws near, he is full of anticipation. Adrenaline is increasing with each breath taken. Unable to wait any longer, he jumps in the car and starts toward the hospital. It is thirty-five minutes early. Waiting in the car at the Walmart parking lot will be easier than sitting around a motel room.

While Moe sits parked in the back of the lot, he notices several cars parking in an area away from the store. The people leaving the cars are walking to the store carrying lunchboxes. The night shift is going to work. Moe's eyes open a little wider as he has an idea. *What's the sense of having my car possibly caught on camera when I can take one of the night shift workers' cars? They won't even know it's gone.*

Time to go. Moe grabs the fire ladders, walks over to a maroon Oldsmobile Cutlass, and within seconds, has the door unlocked. It is a struggle to get the car started. The ignition finally turns over, and Moe is on his way.

At the hospital, Joe looks at Nybo and says, "Ten after ten. They haven't come around to do the ten o'clock wellness check. The only thing that can possibly go wrong is Thelma Lou catching us on camera."

Ten twenty, the roommates are pacing back and forth, often bumping into each other. Neither of them can concentrate. Waiting for the exact moment to act is the hardest part of the plan. Nybo compares the way he feels now with how he felt when he found the dummy in the desert.

At ten twenty-three, Joe slides his bed near their second-floor window and begins tying bedsheets together. As he ties the sheets to the bed frame, Nybo tells him it is not necessary. Joe says, "Let's not change the plan now!"

Nybo states, "Same plan, just follow my lead."

After turning down the power of his gravity shoes, Nybo opens the window and sits on the windowsill. Using the building to push himself forward, he grabs the top of a small tree. The tree bends and gently places him on the ground before up righting itself. Nybo looks up at Joe and says, "Come on, it's easy."

Joe excitedly replies, "Cool, good thinking."

Joe sits on the windowsill and pushes himself off the building. As the tree begins to bend, Joe thinks, *This is fun, what a great idea*. There is a loud snap, and Joe is suddenly lying on the ground with a half a tree on top of him. Other patients hear the snap and look out their windows. They begin yelling for staff. There is no response. As Joe gasps for air, Nybo gets the tree off him. Joe gets up and finds that he must limp to walk.

Thelma Lou returns from the restroom, and the first monitor she sees is the second-floor hall with yelling patients. She calls for additional staff to go there and informs the lone security guard.

Joe and Nybo see taillights back up to the outside of the fence. Moe stands on the car trunk and puts the fire ladders in place. The two escapees work their way across the yard.

As the additional staff calm the patients, the security guard finds the second-floor staff asleep in the break room. Most of them spilled coffee on themselves when the Haldol kicked in.

Reaching the ladder, Nybo helps Joe partway up. Thelma Lou looks away from the second-floor monitor and sees the activity in the yard. She calls for a response from all staff.

Nybo places his gravity shoes on the other side of the fence and gracefully jumps over. Moe climbs the exterior ladder to assist Joe. Staff reach the yard and are running across. Joe slips off the ladder, and his shirt gets caught on the top of the fence. He is helpless, hanging by his shirt. Moe climbs the ladder to assist Joe.

As Joe reaches the ground, Moe says, "Come on. Your turn." Looking into the yard, he says, "Hey, where did he go?"

The staff are nearing the fence. Moe retrieves the ladders and sees Nybo for the first time. Surprised, Moe says, "What the—where did you come from?"

Nybo answers, "Deltoiga."

Joe says, "I told you he's a real alien."

Moe replies, "Yeah, but you didn't tell me he was real. Oh. I guess you did."

As the three pile into the car, the staff reach the fence yelling for them to stop. Additional lights turn on, and a camera zooms in on the car and license plate. The car speeds away.

The trio are almost back to the Walmart as two police cars with flashing lights go flying by on their way to the hospital. Joe says, "Well, they didn't stop us. Where did you get this car?"

Moe replies, "Stole it."

Joe gets a little upset as he says, "You used a stolen car to break us out! Are you nuts?"

Moe reassures Joe by telling him, "Relax. Nobody even knows it's gone. In a couple more minutes, we'll park it right where it was and get into my car."

Joe with relief says, "This isn't your father's Oldsmobile."

Moe says, "You can say that again." The two brothers laugh.

They park the car in the same spot it was taken from. As they begin walking toward Moe's Camaro, Nybo asks about the ladders. Moe tells him, "Just leave them. We'll let the car owner explain them."

Joe again says, "This isn't your father's Oldsmobile."

After piling into the Camaro, Moe says there's a full tank of gas. As the car begins to move, they cheer and say, "Hollywood, here we come." After driving twenty feet, Moe stops the car. Joe asks, "What's wrong?"

Moe answers, "We have a flat tire. Let's work fast."

Joe asks, "Where is the jack?"

Moe impatiently replies, "I don't know. I'm looking for the key to the anti-theft lug nut."

Joe says, "You're a criminal, just figure it out."

Moe responds, "Just find the jack." After several valuable minutes pass, they find the needed items and begin changing the tire.

The police have put out an all-points bulletin on a maroon Cutlass. The flat tire is changed, and the jack is removed. Moe starts tightening lug nuts as Joe places the flat tire in the trunk.

A police car pulls into the lot and stops behind the Cutlass. An officer gets out and talks on the radio attached to his shoulder. The last lug nut is tightened, and everything is placed in the trunk. The officer completes his transmission and spots them as they close the trunk. The officer asks, "You guys okay over there?"

Moe responds, "Yes, sir. Must have been a broken bottle or something. Thanks."

The officer says, "You guys have a good night. Stay out of trouble."

After thanking the officer again, they climb into the Camaro. A second police car, with flashing lights, pulls into the lot. Moe turns the key, and the Camaro makes a grinding sound but does not start. The second police car stops next to the first one, and the officer gets out. Moe tries again, and the Camaro grinds but does not start. The officers look in their direction.

"Third times a charm," says Moe as he turns the key. Third time is a charm. The car starts, and the three are on their way.

Becoming more relaxed now that they are under way, Moe begins a conversation by asking Nybo, "So you really are an alien."

Nybo replies, "Yep."

Moe then states, "I suppose you're going to abduct me."

Nybo replies, "Nope."

Joe says, "I already asked him that."

Moe then asks, "Can I just go with you?"

Joe tells Moe, "I already asked him that too. It was a whole thing about wisdom."

Moe says, "Oh. Huh?"

Back at Walmart, the police have found the owner of the maroon Cutlass. It turns out it was their father's Oldsmobile.

Moe and Joe never knew their father. He left when Moe was two and a half and Joe was one year old. He now lives in Phoenix and works on the night shift at Walmart. There is a lot of explaining to do.

Moe uses his criminal mind to suggest that they stay at the motel tonight. His logic is that the room is paid for, and the cops will be looking for three guys in a car headed out of town. Joe agrees. Nybo is still to jazzed up from all the excitement to know what is going on. Once at the motel, things begin to calm. Nybo steps outside to contact Albie III.

Albie III is relieved to hear from Nybo, and says, "Nybo. I was afraid we might have lost you. It has been a long time since I last heard from you."

Nybo tries to explain. "A lot has been happening, out the window, and the tree, and ladders, the police, and flat tire!"

Albie III is confused and says, "Slow down, Nybo. You're not making any sense."

Nybo is unable to be coherent and continues. "And the tree broke, and Joe, and Moe, and can they come with me, and Pamuhl!"

Albie III jumps out of his seat. "Pamuhl! Did you say Pamuhl?"

Nybo replies, "She's here, Hollywood tomorrow, motel tonight, too many cops, *Wheel of Fortune*."

Albie III says with desperation, "Nybo, you must find her!"

Nybo's mind is moving so fast that he cannot hear anything Albie III is thinking. Nybo states, "Motel tonight, Hollywood, Pamuhl, Spaghetti Betty." A police car speeds by with its siren blaring and lights flashing, and communication is lost. The guys turn in for the night.

A beautiful morning arrives, and the three are up early. Moe asks, "Coffee anybody?"

Nybo excitedly replies, "Ten cups, please."

Joe tells him, "No way. You'll have to stop and pee before we get across the parking lot."

Nybo, realizing he's right, says, "Okay, you're right. Nine cups."

Joe firmly states, "Two cups. And make sure you use the powder room before we leave."

Moe, with a surprised look, says, "The powder room? I'm starting to worry about you, bro."

Joe explains, "They said it on TV last night."

After a short period of getting ready, the three pile into the car. Moe informs them, "It's Saturday, fewer cops on the road. It's around shift-change time. If we avoid donut shops, we should have clear sailing for a couple of hours."

Joe asks, "Do you really think they'll be looking for us? I mean, we're mental, not criminal. It's probably not a big deal to them."

Moe says, "We're not taking any chances. Treat it like we robbed a bank."

Twenty minutes down the road, Nybo says, "I have to go to the bathroom."

Joe raises his voice and says, "What! You did not just say that."

Nybo replies, "Oh, I mean the powder room."

Joe has anger in his voice as he says, "I told you! I knew it. We're not stopping. Pee out the window."

Moe says, "Just hold it. I know a rest area about an hour down the road."

Suddenly, there is a traffic backup. Cars are inching along. After ten minutes, Moe sees what is going on. "It's the cops! They have a roadblock. Holy—"

Joe responds, "If we turn around, it will look suspicious."

Moe states with urgency, "Wait, there's a sign with an arrow. It says, 'Participants.'"

Joe asks, "Participants for what?"

Moe replies, "Not for roadblocks, we're going."

Moe follows the arrow, and after a short drive, they arrive in a parking lot full of decorated cars and floats. There are people wearing costumes. Moe parks away from the activity. Nybo, with relief, says, "I'm going to the powder room now."

Joe tells him, "Pinch it short. We're getting out of here."

Nybo walks across the parking lot to a Porta Potty. As he returns to the car, he is approached by two women. They ask Nybo where he is going. Nybo tells them, "I'm going back to the car. I had to use the powder room."

The women laugh and say, "Oh yeah, you belong in this parade. Let us help you." The girls put lipstick on Nybo and clip small bows onto his earlobes. He returns to the car.

Moe notices Nybo and says, "What the—? What are you doing, ya homo?"

Joe adds, "Whoa."

Nybo explains, "There were some nice girls who helped me."

Moe orders, "Get in before someone sees you."

A small group of parade goers approach the car and ask, "You guys here for the parade?" They see Nybo and say, "Oh yeah, they're here for the parade all right. Here, put these on."

They hand the guys bright-colored, glittery glasses with big eyelashes and feathers. A gay pride flag is attached to the car's antenna, and slogans are painted on the car in washable paint. They state things like, *Baby has three daddies*, and *Once you go gay, you're there to stay.* Turns out the roadblock was to redirect traffic for a gay pride parade.

"You guys are next," they are told.

The Camaro pulls in line behind a gay marching kazoo band. Behind them is a high school marching band followed by Dykes on Bikes. The parade begins. The crowd is waving and cheering. Two guys wearing leather and carrying whips are walking beside them holding hands. A little girl in the crowd recognizes them as her English teacher and dentist. She says, "Hi, Mr. McCarthy. Hi, Dr. White."

They respond, "Hello, Molly, don't forget to do your homework, and don't forget to brush."

"I won't," she promises.

The crowd begins yelling at the guys, "Take it off! Take it off!"

Joe asks, "Take what off?"

Moe says, "Let's start with our shirts."

Joe responds, "Let's end with our shirts."

The three remove their shirts, and people cheer and throw brightly colored beads at them. They put the beads around their necks. They are on their way to Hollywood via a gay pride parade, driving shirtless in a car covered with slogans, wearing colorful glasses and bright beads.

They are driving through a diverse group of people including the mayor, a member of the US Senate, straight people, gay people, some topless people, both men and women. A woman in a costume approaches the car and says, "Hey, daddies, I'll be your baby."

Moe shields his eyes as he says, "Just ignore her. When does this thing end?"

After an hour and ten minutes, the parade route ends. Moe anxiously awaits the opportunity to get back on the road. With the end point in sight, the parade stops. There are two guys getting married to each other. The wedding holds up the parade for twenty minutes.

Several of the other parade goers approach the car and invite the three daddies to the big after party. Nybo is thrilled. "The party will be fun. I hope they have coffee."

Moe says, "Really? We're not going to any party. Especially that one."

Joe says, "I don't know. It might be interesting."

Moe cannot believe it. "What are you talking about, bro? Now I really am worried about you. Besides, I've had enough interesting for one day. One lifetime."

They find the way out and continue their route to the expressway. Two blocks before reaching the entrance ramp, a police car pulls up behind them and turns on the flashers. Joe suggests they make a run for it. Moe says, "Sit tight. When the cop asks for my license, we'll make our move."

The officer approaches the car. The window is already rolled down. He says, "Hey, guys, or gals, or whatever. The parade is over. Do me a favor and put your shirts on. It's illegal to drive without a shirt."

Moe and Joe are relieved as they respond, "Okay, officer, sorry about that."

The officer says, "No problem. Drive safely. See you next year."

With shirts on and beads around their necks, they are on the expressway headed to Hollywood. After a couple of hours of driving through the desert, they stop for a break at a gas station. After putting gas in the car, Moe and Joe go to the restroom. They enter the station and a female clerk says, "Interesting car you got there. You guys gay?"

Moe and Joe insist that they are not gay and go to the restroom. Nybo enters the station.

The clerk asks him, "You guys always drive around with slogans on your car?"

Nybo answers, "Oh no. Those are just there from the parade we were in."

The clerk responds, "Oh. Those are some colorful beads you're wearing. They look like ladies'."

Nybo explains, "People threw them at us when we took our shirts off during the parade."

Moe and Joe return from the restroom. As they are leaving the station, the clerk says with a grin, "You *boyzzz* have a nice day."

Moe says with frustration, "I told you we're not gay."

The clerk responds, "You are straight all right. Straight as a circle."

Moe grumbles and orders, "Let's go. Get in the car."

Driving through the desert is boring. Nybo's mind is busy digesting many of the events he has experienced. He has made attempts to contact Pamuhl but has been unsuccessful.

Joe is counting the number of beads on a necklace. Moe curses the radio while trying to find a consistent signal. From out of nowhere, there is a flying saucer belonging to the Grays hovering above them. Nybo, being overwhelmed by events which have already occurred, takes it in stride.

A blinding light surrounds the car, and it begins shaking. Moe, with concern and confusion, asks, "What the—? What's going on?"

Joe says, "We're being abducted! Finally."

The car is lifted from the ground and drawn toward the saucer. It hangs suspended for a moment before being returned to the road. The flying saucer zips ahead. The Gray pilot had read the slogans on the vehicle and decided that the master race they are trying to build does not include gay people. They are just too nice.

The guys sit stunned on the side of the road and try to digest what has just happened. Nybo states, "That was fun. I was getting really bored."

After several minutes pass, they gather themselves and are ready to resume their journey. A police car pulls up behind them and turns on flashing lights. Moe says, "Oh, great. We would have been better off getting abducted."

Before the officer can exit the car, the flying saucer returns. The police car is surrounded by a blinding light and lifted from the ground. The flying saucer zips away, and the police car is gone. "Easy come, easy go," says Nybo.

While driving the final few hours to Hollywood, Joe and Moe cannot stop talking about the close encounter with the flying saucer. They are driving Nybo nuts. "What does a guy have to do to think around here?" asks Nybo.

"Get a brain," replies Moe.

The three daddies arrive in Hollywood. They decide to get a hotel room for the night where they can form a plan for finding Pamuhl. The car parks in front of the hotel entrance, allowing the desk clerk to read some of the slogans.

Entering the hotel, they are greeted by the desk clerk, "Welcome to Hollywood, you guys will fit right in."

Moe informs the clerk, "We're not gay."

The clerk, who has seen lots of strange things, replies, "No, no."

After renting a room to them, the clerk says, "Hey, listen, you three daddies: no hanky-panky allowed. Other people have to use that room too."

Moe responds, "Agh, we're not gay."

Moe and Joe fall asleep immediately. Nybo steps outside of the room and unsuccessfully attempts to contact Pamuhl. Then he contacts Albie III, who says, "Nybo, have you found Pamuhl? We've been trying to contact her but have not had success."

"I just tried. Nothing. We just arrived in Hollywood. This is where she lives."

"You must find her!"

Nybo says, "We're going to come up with a plan."

Albie III asks, "Who is we?"

"Moe and Joe. They're brothers. Everybody calls us the three daddies."

"What's going on down there?"

Nybo tells him, "We were in a parade to celebrate being gay. It truly was gay; everyone was so happy and having fun. We have to do it on Deltoiga."

Albie III muses, "A gay parade to celebrate being happy, what a great idea." Nybo swats a mosquito and communication is lost. He falls asleep sitting outside.

CHAPTER 10

SPAGHETTI BETTY

Zeta told Pamuhl that he must go. He told her that in the morning a man named Signu would come to escort her across the border. All her fees had been paid by the Black League.

"What fees?" asked Pamuhl.

Zeta explained, "The border is controlled by the cartels. No one comes or goes without the cartel knowing. There's a head fee collected. This time it's six hundred dollars."

Zeta cautioned, "There's danger involved. The Grays have several members in cartels. The cartel will come and check to ensure the proper amount of fees were paid. If anybody speaks to you, just nod. If you must speak, say as little as possible. Keep it to yes or no. The Grays will be looking for you. The last order of business is to come up with an alias. It isn't wise to use your own name. In your case, it could well be suicide. Come up with a few options and discuss them with Signu."

Signu arrived a short time after Zeta departed. "I decided to come this evening so we can leave early," Signu explained. "There are fewer authorities on the US side early in the morning, and the cartel members are usually in a better mood early in the day. You must remain calm at the border. The Grays are exceptional at reading frequencies emitted from bioelectricity. If you feel fear, they'll easily detect it. They get confused by calmness. No matter what happens, no matter what's said, you must remain calm the entire time. Others have failed and were taken away. When that happens, there's nothing we can do to help." After going over details of how things should unfold, Signu asked Pamuhl what her alias is.

"Still working on that one," said Pamuhl.

It was dinnertime on Wednesday night, spaghetti night at the Mexico safe house. Signu and Pamuhl sat down for dinner. They had been searching for an alias for an hour without success. A plate of spaghetti was placed in front of each of them. Pamuhl devoured hers, finishing before the others were half done with theirs. She asked for more, and her wish was granted. Pamuhl quickly downed the second plate. Several of the others had not finished their first plates.

Signu looked at Pamuhl and said, "That's it! Spaghetti Betty! That's your new name." With a spot of sauce on her chin, Pamuhl looked at Signu and grinned widely. There was spaghetti sauce on each corner of her mouth. She broke into a full smile, exposing white teeth half covered in red sauce. As she tilted her head to the left, she said, "Spaghetti Betty, that's me, baby."

In the morning, the exodus began while it was still dark. Signu and Pamuhl were given a fifteen-minute car ride before they were dropped off to join a group of eight other people. It was a twenty-minute walk to the border. Upon arriving they were met by three cartel members carrying guns. The cartel greeted the coyote and counted the people. One of the cartel members said," Something isn't right."

The coyote asked, "What is it?"

"There's something wrong with the fat one." The cartel member pointed at Spaghetti Betty.

Pamuhl somehow remained calm. After a few tense seconds, he said, "We should get paid double for her," and broke out laughing. The group was permitted to cross.

The sun began to rise as the group walked quickly to a road. A large van appeared, and the group squeezed in. There was a fifty-dollar fee for a twelve-minute ride. The Black League had paid for Spaghetti Betty. Signu and Pamuhl were dropped off at the safe house. In the morning, Spaghetti Betty would be on her way to Hollywood, where she would begin her new life.

It was dinnertime on Thursday night. Spaghetti night at the US safe house. Spaghetti Betty enjoyed eating at a dining room table for the last time. When dinner was finished, Signu would depart. He told Pamuhl, "A van will be at the safe house tomorrow morning at eight o'clock sharp. It won't wait any longer than five minutes. There's a schedule to keep. Pickups and drop-offs are made at predetermined times, so there's no room for variations from the schedule. When you reach Hollywood, you'll be dropped off at a predetermined corner at a predetermined time. You'll be met by Xi. The fee for the van ride is three hundred fifty dollars. The Black League has covered the charge."

The van arrived at eight o'clock as planned. The driver, a Mexican American, told Spaghetti Betty to sit in the front seat. "You'll take up too much room in one of the back seats. You're a very large person. Sorry about that. I'm not trying to belittle you." There were several others in the van already. They would be dropped off throughout California and the northwest United States.

As the van rolled along, the driver began speaking to Spaghetti Betty. He told her, "I was once in construction and made a decent living, but the work dried up, and I could not support my family or pay my mortgage. I get over one hundred dollars a head. I always make over a thousand dollars, and sometimes close to two thousand dollars, for a three-day drive. I've been stopped by the police several times, but they don't know what to do, and they don't want to deal with it. They usually just let us go."

The driver told her, "I've been arrested twice but got off both times. What are they going to do, arrest me for giving somebody a ride? They just detain us for a short time and give everyone a court date, then we are on our way. That is why I never allow drugs. Too much risk. It pays very well, but sooner or later, you'll get caught. Besides, drugs are very bad. They'll kill you. Don't do drugs. I had a friend who did drugs. Then he died."

"He overdosed?" asked Spaghetti Betty.

"No, a piano fell him," responded the driver.

The group was approaching San Diego after making several stops throughout the morning. They came to a crawl as traffic was being rerouted. "This better not disrupt our schedule," said the driver.

Once they get near the officer redirecting traffic, the driver asked, "What's going on?"

The officer explained, "There was a group promoting white supremacy who were driving around the area with a loudspeaker making statements about the superiority of the white race and how voting for their candidates will save the country. The driver opened his window to smoke a cigarette and was stung on the neck by a bee. Their van swerved out of control and forced a semi off the road causing it to roll over. Ironically, the truck was hauling a load of honey, which is now cooking on the highway. The white supremacist guys got out of their van slipped and fell. Now they're stuck to the road. The loudspeaker keeps skipping and repeating something about their superior intelligence, and how free they are."

The detour added about seven minutes to their drive, putting them a little behind schedule. The driver became edgy and cursed at other cars on the road. There was no opportunity for passing. Their speed slowed as the line of cars ahead of them grew. An awful odor filled the van, causing everyone to complain and hold their noses. They were stuck in a line of cars following a truck hauling cattle.

As they approached Los Angles, the rush hour was beginning. "We are running very late," said the driver. When the van arrived at the drop-off spot, it was thirty-five minutes past the prearranged time. There was nobody waiting to meet Pamuhl. The driver told her, "Sorry, but I can't wait. You'll have to get out. There's no extra room in the van because of the other pickups I need to make."

Pamuhl was lost and standing on a corner, hoping to be picked up by someone she did not know. This was the first time she had been alone since coming out of the coma. Pamuhl was scared and getting a crash course to being homeless. Sitting on the sidewalk, leaning against a building, she fought to hold back tears. A passerby gives her two dollars. Another passerby told her to take a shower, get a job, and move off the street. She was approached by a missionary, who said, "Good news from heaven, will you take this opportunity to follow the lord?"

Pamuhl responds, "No thanks, I'm waiting for Xi."

A man approached Pamuhl and introduced himself. "My name is Xi. I was here at the prearranged time but left after ten minutes. Normally, if the van hasn't arrived by then, it isn't coming. I thought I'd better check again. Good thing I did. You must be hungry. Would you like something to eat?"

"How about breakfast at Tiffany's?" asks Pamuhl quoting the song.

"How about a Big Mac at McDonald's?" said Xi.

After a quick bite, they walked several blocks to a homeless community. Xi stated, "We got you the best spot we could find. There are more inviting spots, but they're in the undesirable section. Gangs and drugs start on the next block. You get this tent. It's going to get very warm in the middle of the day since there's no shade. You are lucky to be on Earth. Our operation here is better funded than most other planets. We got you a television and a generator. Your new neighbor is Cindy. She'll help you to get accustomed to how things work around here. From this point on, there's no more Pamuhl. You are now Spaghetti Betty."

Cindy stopped by, and Xi introduced them. "You picked a good time to come," said Cindy. "Tomorrow is Panera Bread day. We need to get there early to get the best selection and freshest stuff. The druggies never get up before ten o'clock, if even by then. Wow, you have a cooler. You can use that for a bread box. A TV! Way cool. Do you watch *Wheel of Fortune*?"

Cindy and Spaghetti Betty became close friends over time. Every weekday at six o'clock, the generator was turned on, and a crowd gathered outside of Spaghetti Betty's tent to watch *Wheel of Fortune*. Spaghetti Betty was the best at solving the puzzles.

RETURN TO SENDER

After a good night's sleep, the guys are ready to put their heads together and come up with a plan. Nybo tells the others that he and Albie III have been trying to connect with Pamuhl telepathically but have not had any luck.

Moe shakes his head and says, "I'll pretend that makes sense. We should check the phone book."

Joe responds, "Where are you going to look, in the Alien Pages? How many Spaghetti Bettys can there be? Let's ask around."

Moe looks at Joe in disbelief and says, "That could take days, weeks, forever."

Nybo states, "What would they do on TV? They would probably hire a detective."

Moe and Joe look at each other, and Moe says, "That's not a bad idea."

Joe looks in the yellow pages and finds a private detective. He calls and the detective agrees to meet them at their hotel at two o'clock in the afternoon. The guys decide to spend the morning searching on their own.

As they get ready to leave the room and begin searching, Moe states, "The first thing we do is get the car washed."

Joe hesitates and says, "Think about it for a minute. It's a great disguise. Nobody is looking for three gay guys. It has already gotten us out of trouble."

Moe's face shows that he doesn't like it, but after a second of thought, he says, "You might be right. But one more gay comment from anybody, and it's bath time for the Camaro."

Woody Forest and Autumn Leaf check into the same hotel as the three daddies. The clerk who had checked the guys in is off duty. Nybo and Woody could pass for twin brothers.

Woody and Autumn are now married. It took a long time for Woody to get up the nerve to ask her to marry him. A few years back on a New Year's Eve, the anniversary of the first time they met, Woody overcame his fear and asked, "Would you marry me?"

Autumn smiled widely and excitedly responded, "Would I!"

Woody was half expecting rejection and asked, "Was that Woody, or would I?

Autumn grabbed him, gave him a tight hug, and yelled, "That was yes!" She then added, "Though I think we should wait until you get your first acting gig."

Woody agreed.

Autumn graduated law school and found a job in no time. She had grown impatient waiting on Woody to get an acting gig, so they discarded their plan and got married. They changed the plan from waiting to get married to waiting to drop little acorns.

Woody has now found his first acting gig. A good one. He is a stand-in for a movie being filmed that stars Danny Devito. Autumn has taken a week off from work to come to Hollywood and celebrate with Woody. Woody tells Autumn, "Now we can begin working on little acorns."

"It's about time," she says. "I was afraid the old tree might run out of sap."

Woody and Autumn leave the hotel for breakfast before the main clerk takes over at the desk. The three guys are ready to hit the streets of Hollywood and begin the search for Spaghetti Betty. After the main clerk takes over, the front desk duties, the guys exit the elevator and enter the lobby. The clerk sees them and says, "Good morning three daddies. You guys need to find yourselves some good women." The guys exit the hotel.

Ten minutes later, Woody and Autumn enter the hotel. The main clerk sees them and thinks Woody is Nybo. He draws their attention and smiles and winks at Woody while giving him a thumbs-up. Confused, Woody enters the elevator and says, "I don't think I'm the person you think I am."

"Thank goodness," says the main clerk.

Twenty minutes later, Woody leaves the hotel to go to work. Autumn remains in the room doing legal work. The main clerk becomes confused and is suspicious of some weird sort of sexual activity. The three daddies drive that car, after all.

The guys spend their first morning in Hollywood combing the streets, asking businesses if they know of a large black lady named Spaghetti Betty. A couple of people say they recognize her from *Wheel of Fortune* but have never seen her around.

The guys discover that it does not take long to get discouraged. As lunchtime nears, they stop in a coffee shop for a break. Getting an order to go, they leave the coffee shop. Seconds later, a photo of Nybo appears on the television screen in the coffee shop. The Phoenix police, being aware that Nybo has stated he wanted to go to Hollywood, have contacted several television stations in the Hollywood area and asked them to post a photo of Nybo. The server calls 911.

Woody has been at the studio all morning. Ready for a break, he walks down the street to a high-class restaurant and makes a reservation while thinking, *I'll surprise Autumn with a classy dinner tonight.* Leaving the restaurant, he realizes that he left his wallet in his locker at the studio. *Lunch is out*, he thinks. Searching his pockets, he finds a ten-dollar bill. *A roll and coffee should hold till dinner*, he thinks while entering the coffee shop. Some ICE officers are there talking to the server, who sees Woody enter the shop and points at him while exclaiming, "That's him!"

One of the officers says with surprise, "That is him. You need to come with us, sir."

Woody takes a second to realize they're talking to him and finally asks, "What's going on? What's all this?"

The officer states, "We're taking you back to Phoenix to see Judge Stone."

Woody recognizes that there's a mistake and, without any real concern, explains, "What? I'm not going to Phoenix. I'm an actor."

The officers are aware of Nybo's previous statements about wanting to become an actor. They look at each other, and one of them says, "Oh yeah, this is our guy all right. Hands behind your back, Deltoiga."

Woody is getting confused, but still has no real concern as he says, "Deltoiga? Who is Deltoiga? Who is judge Stone? I'm Woody Forest. I'm an actor. I have to get back to work."

The officer asks, "You have some ID on you?"

Woody tells them "I left my wallet at the studio."

The officer laughs as he says, "Yeah, right. Hands behind your back." Woody is soon handcuffed and sitting in the back of an ICE patrol car headed to Phoenix.

The three guys are headed back to the hotel for their meeting with the private detective. Entering the hotel lobby, they approach the main clerk and inform him they are expecting a guest around two o'clock. They ask him to call their room when their guest arrives.

The clerk is upset and says, "Listen you three daddies, you guys need to knock off the funny business or find a new hotel."

Surprised, Moe asks, "What's the matter?"

The clerk complains, "All this coming and going. Women coming in and not leaving, doing who knows what kind of lewd things. Now another guest."

Moe is confused and says, "I don't know what you are getting at, but I can assure you everything is perfectly normal."

The clerk responds, "It may be normal to you guys, but the rest of the world has moral standards."

Moe is over this conversation and asks, "Could you just call us when our guest arrives?" The three guys go to their room.

At two o'clock, the private detective arrives in the lobby. Walking over to the front desk, he informs the main clerk that he is here to see Joe and his friends. As the main clerk calls their room, he asks the man his name. The detective the guys hired is named Raymond Pist; he goes by Ray. He tells the main clerk, "I'm Ray Pist."

The main clerk lowers the phone from his ear. Someone is speaking on the other end of the line, "Hello, hello, hello? Is anybody there?"

The main clerk gathers himself and says, "There is a rapist here to see you."

Joe replies, "Oh great, send him up. We've been waiting all day for this."

Meeting with Ray Pist was a good idea. Ray knows the Hollywood area and has a vast number of contacts. Ray believes he can find Spaghetti Betty in a short amount of time.

"After all," Ray says, "How many Spaghetti Betty's can there be?" "You guys continue looking also. We should find her within a couple of days."

After some idle chat, Ray leaves while saying, "You guys sure picked a weird hotel. I don't know what's up with that front desk guy, and there's a car in the lot with gay stuff written all over it."

Woody, of course, never returned to the room. Autumn is beside herself with worry. As the hours begin to pile up, she recalls some warnings her coworkers had given her. Her closest friend had said, "It's exciting that Woody will be going to Hollywood to work, but you know there's nothing but perversion there. Everybody cheats on their spouse. Before you know it, he'll stop calling home every day. You'll call him one night, and he won't be there. He'll try to explain it away as working late. If he does come back to you, he'll have so many diseases you won't want to sleep with him."

Autumn is not sure what to think. *Woody loves me*, she decides and calls the police to file a missing person report. She is informed no one is considered missing until after seventy-two hours.

Autumn decides to call a private detective. After calling Ray Pist, who told her he was busy, she called someone else named Richard D. Light, who agreed to meet her at the hotel in the morning.

Morning arrives and the main clerk takes over at the front desk. He sees the three daddies leave the hotel and shakes his head. He feels angry, almost sick, believing that there's weird sexual activity going on.

A man enters the lobby and walks over to the front desk. He introduces himself as Dick D. Light. The main clerk shakes his head and says, "Nooo, no, no, nooo. Your guys aren't here. They just left."

"I'm here to see a lady," says Dick.

The elevator opens, and Autumn steps out and says, "You must be Dick D. Light. Thank goodness you're here. I'm beside myself. I couldn't possibly wait another minute to get started."

Dick informs her, "You were fortunate to catch me at a down time. I'm in high demand."

Autumn smiles and says, "Well then, let's get right at it."

The clerk asks Autumn, "You didn't like Mr. Rapist?"

She replies, "Honestly, I tried him first. He wasn't available. He told me I would not believe the number of requests he gets for his services. He said it would wear most men out, but he has a hard time saying no. I must be the luckiest girl in Hollywood that Dick D. Light could see me today."

Autumn and Dick discuss the situation, and Dick agrees to take the case. "I'll have an answer for you in no time," says Dick. Autumn gives Dick a photo of Woody.

Dick spends the rest of the morning nosing around the studio without success. As he drives down the road, a white Camaro with gay slogans is coming in the other direction. He sees Nybo in the car. Making a harsh U-turn, he forces other cars to swerve. Dick catches up to the Camaro as it is parking in front of a coffee shop. He parks a short distance behind it.

Nybo has become discouraged and is experiencing depression for the first time. Joe is trying to encourage him. They get out of the car, and Joe places his hands on Nybo's shoulders. Nybo looks Joe in the eyes. Dick begins taking photos. "Case cracked," he says to himself as he gets pictures of the car.

Joe tells Nybo he is like a brother and gives him a hug. Dick says to himself, "Here's one for the family album."

Attempting to cheer up Nybo, Moe puts on some of the beads and a pair of the glittery glasses with feathers and joins in on the hug. The camera clicks away.

As the guys walk into the coffee shop, both Joe and Moe put their arms around Nybo. The camera clicks out of control while Dick laughs.

Woody has arrived in Phoenix and is spending the night in a jail cell. He will see Judge Stone tomorrow or the next day. Ray Pist is on to something. He is going to meet the guys in the morning. Dick D. Light returns to the hotel just before the main clerk is about to get off duty. Unable to believe that Dick is back for a second time, the clerk says, "You again? Already?"

Dick smiles and replies, "Yes, sir. Easiest money I ever made."

The clerk shakes his head and mumbles to himself, "I think I'll stop by the church for a while on my way home. And then the bar."

Dick D. Light shows Autumn the photos. She falls into a chair, almost fainting. With tears forming in her eyes, she says, "They said this would happen. I never would have believed it. And so quickly."

Dick, referring to same sex relationships, says, "I'm awfully sorry. Unfortunately, it's all over California these days, especially Hollywood. Here are the photos and my report. If

I'm needed at the divorce, there's an additional fee. Oh, here, I brought you a bottle of whiskey. No extra charge."

Next morning, Autumn is leaving to return to Phoenix with a broken heart. She enters the lobby and approaches the desk. The main clerk sarcastically asks, "So, was Mr. Dick Delight able to satisfy you?"

Autumn replies, "Yes, but I've never been so hurt."

The clerk says with disgust, "Sickening. Some men don't deserve to live."

Autumn is almost in tears and referring to Woody says, "Yes. I was certain I had found the ideal man, and now I feel so empty and used. To think I trusted that man."

The clerk, talking about Dick D. Light, reassures her, "Well, he'll get his. Are you all right? What are you going to do now?"

Autumn answers, "I'm going back to Phoenix to put the pieces back together."

The clerk's voice becomes more uplifted as he says, "Good for you. You've experienced evil ways and have seen the light."

Autumn responds, "Yes, I have. Who thought one's life could be so perverse?"

The clerk states, "I admire your strength. Perhaps you should consider therapy."

Autumn agrees and says, "I believe you're right. I'll start by throwing darts at his picture."

The clerk raises a fist and says, "That's the spirit. Good luck and God bless."

Autumn begins the trek back to Phoenix. Ray Pist enters the hotel for his meeting with the guys. The main clerk is feeling angry and disgusted. He notices Ray heading for the elevator and says to him, "You should be ashamed of yourself, doing what you do for a living."

Ray asks, "Why? All my customers are completely satisfied."

The main clerk informs him, "Not all of them. Some poor gal used a guy named Dick Delight yesterday."

Ray replies, "Oh yes, her. She called me, but I was too busy to be able to do a satisfactory job, so I recommended Dick for her. Dick and I go back a long way. We've been bound together professionally.

The clerk's jaw drops, and he says, "And you talk about it openly?"

Ray calmly answers, "Sure, why not. We're both good at what we do. Just last night, we were at a fling together. Dick told me about her. He said she had a lot of balls to take it the way she did."

The clerk is now in shock as he says in disbelief, "My God!"

Ray informs him, "It's sad, but you would be amazed at how often this type of thing happens."

Ray arrives at the room and knocks on the door. "Good morning, gentlemen," he says as he sits down. "I put out some feelers yesterday, and my contacts came through."

Ray hands Joe a piece of paper with an address. "This is what Spaghetti Betty has been using for an address. She has a post office box there. The street address belongs to a shipping and packing business. They say Spaghetti Betty comes to check her box two or three times each month. We found it because she sold the car that she won on *Wheel of Fortune* to a car lot belonging to one of my contacts."

Joe excitedly responds, "That's great!"

Ray replies, "Not really, it isn't over yet. Now the only thing to do is keep the place under surveillance until she comes to check her mail. You can pay me to do it, or you can do it yourselves. Frankly, I don't have the time. It has been over two weeks since she last checked it, so it shouldn't be long before she shows up."

Woody will see Judge Stone in the morning. He has been trying to reach Autumn without success. Woody leaves a message each time, telling her when he will be in court and asking her to represent him. Autumn arrives in Phoenix and checks her messages. After hearing them, she is confused and doesn't understand what is happening.

Autumn wants a divorce; she has the photos after all. But how did Woody get to Phoenix, and why is he going to court? "Probably in trouble for another one of his sex romps," she says to herself. Autumn decides she will go to the hearing. Where is there a better place to serve divorce papers? Maybe it will help her to understand what happened.

The morning of the hearing, Judge Stone lets his dog out before heading into court. A car driving much too fast strikes the dog and instantly kills it. Autumn, in her grief and haste, was not paying attention while driving to the courthouse. Stopping the car, she feels terrible. Getting out of the vehicle, she tells Judge Stone how horrible she feels and how sorry she is. She explains how her life has been turned upside down.

Judge Stone is both grieved and shocked. He angrily tells Autumn to get in her car and leave. There is no time to bury the poor dog now—it'll have to wait till this evening. So, the judge goes to work in a dejected state.

The first case of the day is the one involving Nyboa Deltoiga. Judge Stone can't believe it and says, "I should have stayed home. Mr. Deltoiga, you seem to have gotten yourself into quite the pickle."

Woody attempts to explain, "Your Honor, I have no idea who this Deltoiga guy is. I'm an actor."

Judge Stone is already in a bad mood and states, "Don't even start with me today. I see you brought the counsel in your head again."

Woody replies, "With all due respect, Your Honor, there's nothing in my head. My counsel isn't in the courtroom."

Judge Stone says, "Maybe Dr. Colgate did you some good after all."

Woody asks, "What are you talking about? Are you okay?"

Judge Stone states angrily, "Mr. Deltoiga, I'm really not in the mood for your shenanigans today. You have some serious issues to deal with."

Autumn quietly opens the door and enters the courtroom. Woody is frustrated and continues to try and explain, "I told you: I'm an actor. I need to get to Hollywood."

The courtroom door slams shut. Everyone in the courtroom turns and sees Autumn, including Judge Stone. Woody smiles and says with relief, "Ahh, my counselor is here."

Judge Stone suddenly recognizes Autumn and states very loudly, "*You!*"

Woody asks, "You two know each other?"

Judge Stone informs him, "Mr. Deltoiga, you should have stuck with the counsel in your head."

Woody, feeling more confident now that Autumn has arrived, says, "I'm Woody Forest and this is my counselor, Autumn Leaf."

Judge Stone is now fed up and says, "Woody Forest and Autumn Leaf. And I'm the Jolly Green Giant, except today I'm not too jolly. I've heard enough. First, I'm giving you three days for contempt of court."

Autumn says, "I'll wait for you."

Judge Stone continues. "Based on Dr. Colgate's analysis and your lack of respect for this court, I have contacted the Mexican authorities to inform them you are being deported back to Mexico. They have ways of dealing with mental health criminals."

Autumn states, "Well, not now. Here are some divorce papers for you. Have fun with the sexual weirdos in Mexico."

Woody is confused and in disbelief as he says, "Autumn! It's all a big mistake." He is taken out of the courtroom and placed in jail for the next three days.

Back in Hollywood, the three guys are about to leave the hotel to begin the stakeout. An agent from the studio stops by to deliver Woody's pink slip and last paycheck. The main clerk observes the man hand the check to Nybo and hears him say, "You sure know how to blow it." The main clerk hangs his head and shakes it.

CHAPTER 12

SEARCHING BROWNYWOOD

Nybo enters the bank that issued the check to Woody Forest. Upon reaching the front of the line at the teller window, he is greeted with a good morning and a smile. The teller recognizes Nybo as Woody and, referring to the movie, asks how the project is going. Nybo, referring to the search for Pamuhl, responds that there was a big breakthrough, and now the end is in sight.

The teller replies, "Good for you," and asks for identification.

Moe instructed Nybo to tell them he forgot his wallet, and gave him several stories to explain why he really needs the cash now. Nybo relates them to the teller, "The money for the producer's kid's school fundraiser is due today, and I owe the director some cash that I promised to pay back today. And I need to buy a bouquet of flowers for a birthday. This is the day I buy food for the homeless. They depend on me."

The teller explains the policy that requires identification whenever receiving cash is involved. Checking Woody Forest's account, the teller says, "Well, you have enough to cover it, and I do know who you are."

Nybo leaves the bank with a few thousand dollars and three cups of coffee. Moe and Joe are very excited about the money. Moe states how fortunate it is to get the cash, since his stash is getting low. Moe and Joe thank Nybo for getting coffee. Nybo says, "Oh, did you want some?"

After getting supplies for the stakeout, they locate the address. There is not an available parking space anywhere. Moe drops Joe and Nybo off to observe the building from the sidewalk across the street, then parks at a parking garage three blocks away.

A bench is available, so they are fortunate to sit rather than stand or sit on the sidewalk leaning against a building. The street is filled with litter. Flattened cans and paper cups lay in the street. Pieces of paper blow by a man lying down on the sidewalk a half block away. Occasional gusts of wind bounce sand and dirt off the guy's faces.

Moe walks across the street and checks the store hours. He reports to the others the store is open from 7:00 a.m. to 8:00 p.m. but closed on Sunday. Joe states that getting there at 6:00 a.m. tomorrow will hopefully allow them to get a parking spot.

Eight o'clock arrives, and the store closes. Joe says, "I didn't know sitting all day was such hard work."

At six o'clock in the morning, the guys find a great parking space for the stakeout. There are lingering homeless walking in the area, though most have cleared out for the day. A man is urinating on the wall of a business. A woman takes a drink from a bottle inside of a paper bag. After holding the bottle to her mouth for several seconds, she holds it upside down and shakes it before tossing it onto the street. A dog with his ribs sticking out passes by.

By six forty-five, the remaining homeless have cleared out. A few of the business owners begin to sweep and hose off the sidewalks in front of their shops. Moe reads the newspaper he brought to help pass the time. "A lot going on in the world," he says.

Nybo asks, "Where is the world?"

Moe answers, "The world is the earth."

Nybo says, "Oh. Where is the earth?"

Moe says, "Seriously? What planet do you think you are on?"

Nybo replies, "The United States of America."

Both Moe and Joe laugh before explaining how the United States is part of the earth. Nybo is confused and tells them, "Part of my mission is to let your leaders know that Deltoiga hasn't seen Anyone."

Moe asks, "What are you talking about?"

Nybo says, "You know, the message your leaders keep sending, asking if the voyager Anyone is out there."

After Moe explains how the message is not about a missing astronaut, but about searching for life in outer space, he says, "I guess the message worked. Although I believe they were expecting to receive a message in return, not an actual visit. If they knew you were here, they would hold you in Area 51 and run all kinds of tests on you to find out about your genetic makeup."

Joe states, "You know, when you think about it, it sounds a lot like the Grays."

By noon, the guys are going crazy from boredom. Joe goes down the street to a diner and brings back some hamburgers. Halfway through the burgers, Nybo chokes as he says, "That's her!"

A large black woman pushing a shopping cart enters the shipping store. She exits and Nybo charges toward her with his arms open ready to embrace her. Just as he begins to say her name, she screams and shoots chemical spray into his eyes while shouting, "Get away from me, you little cracker!"

Joe runs toward them and yells, "What's wrong with you, yah psycho?" He then places his hands over his eyes as he feels the burn of the chemical spray in them.

Spaghetti Betty throws the empty spray container, bouncing it off Joe's head. Moe decides he better hang back to assist the others. Spaghetti Betty walks away, pushing her cart and mumbling, "This neighborhood sure has gone downhill since the crackers started moving in."

Time for a new plan. "Obviously, she can't live to far from the shipping store since she walked to it pushing a shopping cart," deducts Moe. "Why was she pushing a shopping cart anyway? Maybe she's homeless. Nybo, you didn't drag us halfway across the country to look for some homeless person? It's hard to believe an alien astronaut would come to Earth and end up homeless in Hollywood."

Nybo responds, "That's Pamuhl all right. I might have gone about things the wrong way today."

A decision is reached to walk around the area to look for Pamuhl. Joe says, "And we don't have to get there at six in the morning."

Nybo contacts Albie III, who says, "Greetings Nybo."

Nybo replies, "Hello, Albie III. I'm a little confused, but if I understand things right, the United States of America isn't a planet at all. It's a country on a planet called Earth. All those other planets, like Mexico and Honduras, they're countries on Earth also."

Albie III responds, "Now you're confusing me. Any word on Pamuhl?"

Nybo tells him, "Yes! We found her today."

Albie III excitedly asks, "Why didn't you say so? How is she?"

Nybo replies, "I don't know. I didn't get to talk to her. She sprayed something into my eyes and called me names."

Albie III instantly falls from a state of excited elation to depression. Confused, he says, "What! You found her and didn't even talk to her. Oh, Nybo. They all said you were the wrong person for this mission." Albie III is distraught and unable to maintain communication.

Parking in the same garage where Moe parked the first day of the stakeout, the guys exit the vehicle, and the search begins anew. It does not take long to be in a homeless community.

"Watch where you step," says Moe.

Joe says, "Yeah, there are used needles everywhere."

Moe responds, "I was talking about the piles of feces."

A man wearing a safety vest and respirator mask is cleaning feces off the sidewalk before spraying the spot down with sanitizing water. They ask him if he has seen a large black woman pushing a shopping cart. "You just described half the people here," he replies.

Nybo asks why there's so much poop in Hollywood. The man replies, "We don't call it Hollywood anymore. We call it Brownywood."

Within two blocks, there is a homeless community in a large field next to a church. As the guys enter the community and start inquiring about Spaghetti Betty, they are approached by a man and woman who introduce themselves as security. After a short discussion, the security force is convinced that the guys are not there to sell drugs.

The guys are told that nobody in the community goes by Spaghetti Betty. "We just moved our community here a couple of weeks ago. We aren't allowed to stay in one spot for more than a year. We really haven't met a lot of the freelance homeless in the area. There's a four-block section of tents lining both sides of the street if you go that way," the woman says and points.

Moe says how impressed he is that there's security. The woman says, "It's a requirement of living in this community that no one does drugs and everyone participates in security shifts."

The guys walk for a block before reaching the stretch of tents. A man sitting on the curb is injecting opioids into his arm. Once finished with the needle, it is discarded on the street ten feet from a hazardous waste disposal box.

A dog barks from inside one of the tents as they pass by. A woman approaches them and asks, "Yawl got a cigarette I can borrow?" After being informed that none of the three smoke, she asks, "How about five dollars? Can you give me five dollars?" Nybo hands her a ten and asks for change. She tells him, "Come back tomorrow and I'll have it for you." The guys ask her about Spaghetti Betty, and she tells them she is not familiar with anyone by that name.

Each block they walk has less piles of feces and discarded needles. They are getting away from the bad section and nearing where Spaghetti Betty's tent is located. "This is crazy," says Nybo.

Joe responds, "Yeah, why doesn't somebody do something?"

A homeless woman hears them and laughs. "What are they going to do, evict us? If they evict one of us, they must evict all of us, everyone throughout the city. Besides, cops won't come here anyway, even if you call them."

The homeless woman turns out to be Cindy. Spaghetti Betty is inside her tent and hears the guys asking Cindy about her. Cindy asks, "Who wants to know?"

"Just a friend from the old neighborhood," says Joe.

Convinced that the guys must be Grays, Spaghetti Betty grabs a Taser. Cindy calls to Spaghetti Betty. The tent door is opened, and the Taser appears. Moe is suddenly on the sidewalk, flopping around like a fish out of water. Nybo yells, "Pamuhl! Pamuhl! I have come from Deltoiga. I'm here to take you home!"

Spaghetti Betty asks, "How do I know you're not Grays?"

Joe excitedly says, "Yes! More proof they're real." Moe groans from down on the sidewalk.

Nybo rapidly begins making his case. He explains how Albie III is his wisdom guide and the son of Albie II. Nybo tells her the name of her old spacecraft, the *Albie*, and how he grew up next to the Edelsons. "I was the one that ruined Mrs. Edelson's night lily garden just before the celebration."

Spaghetti Betty, now Pamuhl again, invites Nybo into her tent. A small crowd begins to form outside the tent to see what the ruckus is about. Joe is assisting Moe into Cindy's tent. The crowd hears the conversation between Spaghetti Betty and Nybo.

Pamuhl says, "Show me who you are, little cracker." Nybo changes into his natural Deltoigan form. Pamuhl lets out a loud "Whew," and says, "I'm sorry I doubted you."

Nybo responds, "Now you show me something."

Pamuhl tells him, "It's been a long time, sugar, but I'll see what I can do." She takes a second and then changes to her natural Deltoigan form.

Nybo says joyously, "I don't think I've ever seen anything so beautiful."

Both Nybo and Pamuhl are laughing and giggling, letting out yahoos, and saying things like, "Oh my God," and, "I can't believe this is really happening." After a couple of minutes pass, Pamuhl thanks Nybo. She states, "I never thought this day would come. I can't believe what you've done for me."

Nybo replies, "You have no idea how relieved I feel right now." As the crowd outside claps and cheers, Zeta stands behind them, wondering what is happening.

As the two Deltoigans change back into their human forms, Zeta stands near the tent door and calls out for Spaghetti Betty. Joe, now standing between two tents, with a friend in each one, says to Zeta, "I don't recommend standing there. She has a lot of tricks up her sleeve."

Pamuhl opens the tent and sees Zeta. Surprised she says, "Zeta! What are you doing here? I didn't expect to see you. Then again, I didn't expect to see anyone from Deltoiga either."

Zeta says, "We need to talk. We need to get you out of here."

CHAPTER 13

NOW WHAT?

Woody Forest is headed to Mexico on an ICE bus. He will be handed over to the authorities and is considered mentally ill and dangerous.

Autumn Leaf has begun therapy.

The main clerk at the hotel now keeps a flask of liquor under the desk.

Nybo cannot wait to squeeze into the spacecraft with Pamuhl and get back to Deltoiga.

Moe and Joe are in Cindy's tent, asking her to keep that crazy lady, Spaghetti Betty, away from them. Zeta enters Pamuhl's tent and says, "You have been very foolish. What were you thinking, using your own name on national television?"

Zeta explains, "The Grays have a cold-case system they use to try and locate subjects they have lost track of. In the first two years, a subject's name appears in their system several times. By the third year, it may only be a couple of times. After that, it may be less than annually."

He tells her, "When you slipped up by using your real name on *Wheel of Fortune*, you were surely spotted by a Gray or one of their abductees who now work for them on Earth. A red flag entered into their system would have bumped your name up toward the top of the cold-case list."

Nybo is confused. He has heard of the Grays through Joe but is unaware of Pamuhl's experience with them. Pamuhl asks, "You really think the Grays are going to try and find me because of that?"

Zeta responds, "You should know that their cranial capacity is two and a half times that of humans. If these guys could find you, the Grays won't have any problem."

Moe and Joe are concerned about Nybo. Joe suggests they go to Spaghetti Betty's tent and check on him. Moe agrees and begins looking for something to hit her with if she should try to spray or Taser them.

Cindy convinces them it will be all right now that Spaghetti Betty knows they are friendly. Cindy stands in front of Spaghetti Betty's tent door and calls for her. Moe and Joe stand far off to the side.

Pamuhl, Nybo, and Zeta emerge from the tent. Following introductions, and explaining who's who, Zeta tells everyone that things have gotten complicated, and they need to find somewhere private to hash things out.

Pamuhl recommends the library. "It isn't raining today, so it won't be crowded and shouldn't smell too bad," she says, explaining how the homeless use it for a shelter during stormy and cold weather.

Cindy states, "This time of day, the mass transit system isn't as busy, and the homeless won't be sheltering there either. We should be able to find a semiprivate car."

"Wait," says Moe. "Let's go to the hotel. We can all squeeze into the Camaro. It's only a short drive." Zeta reluctantly agrees, and the six of them, including the enormous Spaghetti Betty, cram into the Camaro.

Zeta, after seeing the car, asks, "You guys are gay, huh?"

Moe responds, "We're not gay!"

Zeta moves a pair of the glitter glasses from the seat so he can sit down. "One of you guys lost your glasses," he says.

Moe responds, 'We're not gay."

Pamuhl and Cindy each put on a pair of the glitter glasses and say, "Hey, everybody, look at us. We're gay." They let out a loud laugh.

At the hotel, the main clerk sees the gang pile into the elevator. Pamuhl and Cindy are still wearing the glitter glasses. When the door slides shut, the liquor flask is removed from under the counter, and the main clerk takes a big swig.

Once in the room, Zeta becomes very serious. He gets angry at the group and tells them, "This isn't a game. Pamuhl is in grave danger, and now so are the rest of you."

Zeta explains, "Pamuhl, the location of your tent isn't so random as you think. The building behind you is a microwave-manufacturing facility. Perhaps you've noticed that your television reception improves greatly after six o'clock when the factory closes."

Pamuhl responds, "Just in time for *Wheel of Fortune*, baby."

Zeta continues. "Yes, just in time for *Wheel of Fortune*. The electronic frequencies emitted and the radioactive emissions interfere with the Grays' searching techniques."

Nybo says, "That's why nobody from Deltoiga has been able to reach you. That's why I have not been able to communicate with you telepathically."

Zeta responds, "That's right. Did you notice a drone fly over while we were standing outside of the tent? That was the Grays. The Goodwill guy delivering water to the tents—I'm 90 percent sure he reports to the Grays. I'm afraid they've located Pamuhl. Now we must act quickly, as you're all in their sights. There's very little time."

Cindy asks, "Who are all you people? What's going on here? Who are Pamuhl and the Grays? What's this Deltoiga? Take me back to my tent. C'mon, Spaghetti, we're leaving."

Zeta recognizes her stress and says, "I'm sorry. There isn't time to explain now. You must trust us. You are in very real danger. If the Grays get ahold of you, they'll put you through some torturous test and then either use you for hard labor or eat you. Unfortunately, you were caught with the wrong people at the wrong time. Things are changing for the worse very rapidly. The Grays have become more aggressive and started doing strange things. Their plot to take over Earth appears to have started. There's a safe house on an Indian reservation up north. We must leave for it now, and I mean now."

Cindy says, "You think we're going to drive around with six people in a Camaro?"

Moe looks at Pamuhl and says, "You could say seven."

Pamuhl responds, "Don't make me spray your cracker behind." She then asks, "How are we going to squeeze eight people in there?"

Joe says, "Don't belittle yourself. It doesn't fit you," and starts laughing.

Pamuhl responds, "Oh, that's it, baby. Where's my spray at?"

Zeta says, "Please stop. I'll make a phone call. We'll have another car here in minutes. Please don't spray anyone."

Nybo insists it is time to return to his spacecraft and take Pamuhl back to Deltoiga. Zeta tells him it's too risky to go directly there. "We must sit tight at the safe house for two or three days till we can be sure the coast is clear."

The others have no desire to go to a safe house. Cindy does not want to go anywhere but is convinced by Pamuhl that it is for her own good. Besides, she finds both Moe and Joe attractive.

Zeta has arranged for a car big enough to comfortably fit the six of them. Joe tells the story of how the police car was abducted in the desert and how close they were to being abducted themselves. Zeta gets a shocked look on his face and asks, "Why wasn't I told about this before?" He then muses, "Of course! The Grays do not understand or tolerate homosexuals. You guys are fortunate to be gay."

Moe groans and says, "We're not gay."

After Joe explains how the phrases on the Camaro got there, and about the beads and glasses, Zeta gets excited. "We'll paint the new car the same way. What a great disguise."

The new car arrives, complete with gay sayings similar to those painted on the Camaro. The three aliens and Joe ride in the new vehicle while Moe and Cindy follow in the Camaro. Moe explains to Cindy about Nybo and Pamuhl being aliens.

In the other vehicle, Joe says, "Holly cow, I'm in a car with three actual aliens. I didn't even have to leave Earth."

Nybo is brought up to snuff on what happened to Pamuhl and how she ended up living in a tent on the streets of Hollywood. Zeta explains how the Grays place a chip in the shoulder of their abductees and anyone else they wish to control. "We are able to deactivate the chip but not always completely. That's why the precaution was taken to set up

Pamuhl next to the microwave factory. The safe houses we use are designed to interfere with the Grays' ability to track the chip's signal and to stop them from controlling the individual with the shoulder chip."

"Where is this safe house?" asks Joe.

Zeta responds, "In Utah. Eventually, we'll be going to one in Arizona. Then we can take Nybo and Pamuhl to their spacecraft. It's too risky to go directly there. My sources have informed me that the route between California and Arizona is being heavily surveilled by the Grays right now. The entire southwestern United States is a hotbed for Gray activity. There's an entire underground system complete with extremely fast transportation. They discovered a mixture of hydrogen, oxygen and other minerals which produces combustion capable of propelling them beyond light speed. We'll be heading right into the heart of their territory. Hopefully, they won't expect that. Let's hope our vehicle decorations work."

"They will," says Joe. "You can trust me on that." Nybo agrees.

The vehicles are traveling northeast when they pass a billboard for a business called Alien Jerky. Pamuhl gets excited and asks if they can stop there. Nybo does not think it's such a good idea since the jerky could be made from aliens.

Joe explains that it is just a business name and the jerky isn't made from aliens. Zeta asks, "What's it made from?"

Joe responds that he does not know for sure, "Probably cow or pig or something." The others decide jerky is not a good idea.

Moe and Cindy are developing feelings for each other and building a relationship. Cindy explains how she was once addicted to drugs, which had caused her to be kicked out of a friend's house, leaving her nowhere to go. She ended up in prison, where she was required to attend treatment, and has been off drugs ever since. While Moe tells Cindy about losing his job and about how he has been in and out of prison, their hands clasp.

A bear runs across the road in front of them. Joe gets excited and asks, "Did you see that?" The aliens ask what it was, and Joe explains bears to them before stating, "I wouldn't want to tangle with one."

Stopping at a rest area, Joe and Moe use the restroom. Nybo decides to have fun and changes to a bear form. As Joe exits the restroom, he sees the bear and starts screaming while running to a flagpole. Once he has climbed halfway up the pole, Nybo returns to human form. Nybo and Pamuhl laugh while Joe climbs down the pole, cursing. "That's not funny," he says, "Someone could have a heart attack."

Zeta shakes his head and asks, "Can we please be serious?"

Joe sees a billboard advertising the Old Woman Meteorite. Becoming very excited, he asks about stopping to see it. The three aliens in the vehicle look at each other before Zeta says, "It's a rock, Joe. The less we stop, the better. We'll stop in Vegas for gas and a brief break; that's it."

After driving through the desert for several hours, the group reaches the top of a hill, and the lights of Las Vegas appear. Stopping for gas, Zeta tells everyone to stick together. On their way to the restroom, Pamuhl and Cindy pass by a woman at a slot machine. The woman tells them that she has a bad gambling problem, so her husband does not allow her to go to casinos anymore. "He hasn't figured out why I go to the gas station every day for cigarettes," she says.

Two men are snorting lines of cocaine from off the checkout counter when the owner sees them and begins yelling and telling them to leave. The men reply, "This is Vegas. It's okay." The owner informs them that drugs are illegal everywhere, including Las Vegas.

When the ladies come out of the restroom, the woman at the slot machine is gone. Pamuhl slips a coin in and hits the jackpot. A light flashes, and a bell rings continuously. Zeta hears the bell and sees Pamuhl being approached by the owner. The owner gives her a certificate to take to a nearby casino where she can claim her prize. He informs her she will need to show her Social Security card.

Zeta takes her arm and escorts her out to the car. "What are you doing?" he asks. He reminds the group that they are not to call attention to themselves.

"What you just did was very foolish. They'll check the security camera and see you."

The group leaves the station. Joe says he has a Social Security card. They somehow talk Zeta into claiming the money. Joe and Moe enter the casino and head to the cashier window. Outside, a man looks over the vehicles and snaps a photo with his phone. Zeta states, "We've been had." The guys return with a couple thousand dollars, and the group hurries out of Las Vegas.

After driving several hours, the gang makes another stop for gas. Zeta again reminds everyone to stick together and not call attention to themselves. He tells them, "No more goofing around."

Joe goes to the restroom, which is accessed from an outside door at the back of the station. When he exits, there is a bull standing near the corner of the building. The bull drops and lifts his head with a snort, then stomps his foot. Joe says, "Come on, Nybo, knock it off. Zeta said no more goofing around."

Joe then walks toward the bull to get around the building. The bull gets confused by Joe's lack of fear and stands still, watching him. Joe sees Nybo sitting in the car and looks back at the bull that is still watching Joe. Letting out a scream, Joe runs to the car, with the bull following close behind. Joe runs around the car before getting in. The bull runs up to the car, veering away once he is near. Zeta again gets upset and sternly asks, "Why must you people insist on calling attention to yourselves?"

Twenty miles down the road, a drone begins following the two vehicles. Zeta states, "I knew this would happen."

After an hour, a black SUV begins to follow them. They reach a tunnel, and partway through, Zeta stops. "Get out of the car, quickly!"

The black SUV is owned by the Black League and stops behind them. The group swaps vehicles. Moe protests, "I'm not leaving my Camaro!"

Zeta responds, "It will be available when you need it. If we're to get through this, you must listen to me and follow instructions. You people seem to think this is just a game."

The vehicles exit the tunnel. The Camaro and other vehicle the gang were using turn at the first exit they come to, taking the drone with them. The group remains on the road and continues their trek. Upon reaching a mountain range, Zeta turns onto a rough, unmaintained road that takes them to a cave. Driving into the cave, they are greeted by several Black League members holding weapons.

CHAPTER 14

WHAT ABOUT DELTOIGA?

The group stands in a dimly lit cave that is protected by Black League members holding strange-looking weapons. Following brief introductions, Zeta goes into a room with the commander. The rest of the group remains at the cave entrance whispering among themselves. Joe is in awe as he says, "Look at all these aliens."

Moe is scared and says, "I don't like this. I think they're taking us prisoner. I mean we don't even really know this Zeta guy."

Nybo agrees, "I do have a strange feeling about this."

Cindy says, "Let's get out of here."

Moe responds, "We can't run. They took the Camaro. I'm afraid we're at their mercy."

Pamuhl is not sure how to feel. While trying to make sense of things, she says, "They've taken care of me for twelve years. All the Grays did was put me in a coma and drop me off in Mexico. I think we can trust them."

A tall, slender, human-looking woman approaches the group. After introducing herself as Ursa, she says, "You all must be tired and hungry. Come with me." They follow her into a brightly lit room and are seated at a dining table. Ursa asks if anybody would like some dinner. "We're having spaghetti tonight," she says.

"Whew, bring it on," says Pamhul.

During dinner, Ursa tells the group, "I'm sure you have lots of questions. I can answer basic questions, but for your own good, there are a lot of things that must be on a need-to-know basis."

Moe asks," Why is it so bright in here?"

Ursa explains," The reptilian Grays have sensitive eyes. Bright lights and sunshine are things they try to avoid. You rarely see them outside during the day without dark glasses unless it's heavily overcast. They're still uncomfortable in the sun, even with the dark glasses. The brightness within the cave is a security measure."

Zeta enters the room and joins in the meal. Pamuhl starts on her second plate. Zeta asks, "Has Ursa been able to explain things to you?"

"She's doing that now," says Joe. "What's this place?"

Ursa tells them they are in the west region headquarters of the Black League Resistance, known as the BLR. "Zeta was wise to bring you here rather than allowing you to go to your spacecraft. The Grays are cleaning up a lot of loose ends, like their cold-case system, in preparation for their takeover of Earth. They don't want any distractions when they reveal to the world who they are. You wouldn't have made it to your spacecraft."

Nybo looks at Ursa's short brown hair bounce as she explains the Grays' history with Earthlings. How they instantly figured out human greed and used it against them when bargaining with world leaders. She tells them that Hitler was one of the first world leaders they bargained with; he traded Jews in concentration camps for technology. The Grays bargained with the United States at the same time, but the United States demanded humane treatment of abductees, where Hitler did not care how the Jews were treated. Eventually, Hitler's insanity became too much for the Grays to handle, so in the end, they helped destroy him by providing technology to the United States and their allies.

Nybo gazes at Ursa's long fingers as her hands move while she tells the group, "The Grays have already started their war on America. By controlling world leaders through hypnosis and inserting chips in them, the Grays have been systematically distracting and destroying the United States. Once they control the United States, they'll bring down China and Russia. The Grays infiltrated the cartels and gave them the recipe for Phytanoyl so they could sell it to Americans to dumb down and numb a large portion of the population to make the takeover that much easier. So many United States leaders have had their lust for wealth and power used against them. They were deceived into believing they would dominate the world along with the Grays. They won't, but through their greed, they will obey the wishes of the Grays, believing they will reap the benefits. The Grays will likely eat them in the end. For now, the Grays are using them to keep the southern border open so the drugs can continue to easily flow into the United States. They never expected a nonpolitician to become leader. They have no control over him, which is one of the reasons they're stepping up their takeover plan."

Ursa continues, stating, "China was able to capture one of the Grays' pilots after a crash occurred. There was an agreement made with China which gave them advanced technology in exchange for the pilot, as well as open abductions." She continues. "The Grays have sold out the United States. The world leaders foolishly believe that they can win a war against the Grays. The leaders forget that their most destructive and efficient weapons come from the technology given to them by the Grays. The Grays know the shortcomings of all the weapons. Weapons used by the Grays are developed with far superior technology."

Nybo asks, "How do you know this?"

Zeta replies, "The BLR is made of several different types of aliens, including Grays and humans. We have spies and double agents working closely with the Grays. Many are working in their underground system. With your ability to change forms, you and Pamuhl would be of great service to us, along with the rest of you."

Nybo responds, "Thanks for the offer, but I'm just going to take Pamuhl back to Deltoiga and complete my mission."

Pamuhl says, "I do miss Deltoiga. Unfortunately for me, I'll be returning home without completing my mission. Gone twenty years and I return a failure."

Zeta asks Pamuhl what her mission was. When she explains it was to chart stars and planets, Zeta and Ursa look at each other with concern. Nybo recognizes it and asks them what's wrong. Zeta says to Pamuhl, "The Grays confiscated your spacecraft."

She acknowledges they did. Zeta continues. "The charts you were developing were in the spacecraft."

Pamuhl again confirms that was the case. Zeta turns a little pale as he says, "Don't you see? Those charts are like handing them a map to Deltoiga!"

Pamuhl says, "We must get back to Deltoiga right away! Take us to the spacecraft."

Ursa responds, "Don't be foolish. You will be walking right into their hands. That won't save Deltoiga or help anyone but the Grays."

Nybo states that he has been unsuccessful at trying to contact Albie III lately. "You don't think they destroyed Deltoiga, do you? I'll try again right away."

Zeta recommends that everyone stay calm. "Whatever has already happened, has happened. There's nothing we can do about it. We don't know about Deltoiga, but if anything has happened there, we can't change it now. Let's stay calm and keep cool heads. It's possible that nothing has happened."

Nybo is taken to a quiet area away from the cave so he can try to reach Albie III. After several tries, he succeeds. Albie III is in good spirts as he says, "Ah, Nybo, there you are. We were just talking you."

Nybo asks, "We?"

Albie III informs him, "Lots has been happening while you've been away. We have guest from another planet called Betelgeuse who are the most interesting and helpful people. They're sharing some incredible technology with us. They're taking some of our citizens to tour their planet."

Nybo in a panic warns, "No! Albie III don't believe them!"

Albie III says, "Don't be silly, Nybo. They're very helpful and teaching us how to keep our planet habitable. They're very interested about you and what has happened to Pamuhl. They were wondering if you were able to contact her. Have you?"

Nybo becomes weak from the sickening feeling that suddenly has rushed through his body. Feeling like he might faint, he again tries to warn, "Albie III, don't believe them. They aren't the nice people you think they are. If they take some of our citizens to tour their planet, they won't return. If they do return, they'll have been converted to spies."

Albie III lets out a little laugh and says, "What are you talking about, Nybo? They have given us so much. I think you have been away for a little too long."

Nybo feebly tries one last warning, "Albie III, they're trying to take over Deltoiga. They're trying to rule over all planets and living beings."

Albie III sighs and says, "The Wisdom Core members all said you were wrong for this mission, though they never thought you'd go wacko. Come home, Nybo, and meet our new friends. Nybo? Nybo, are you there? Nybo?" Nybo cannot answer and loses his concentration.

Retuning to BLR headquarters, Nybo reunites with the others. Along with Zeta and Ursa, there is a BLR major in the room. As Nybo relates his conversation with Albie III to the them, Pamuhl begins crying and says, "This is all my fault."

The Major replies, "You mustn't blame yourself. You were doing your job. It's not your fault." Zeta introduces the man as Major Canis, who continues. "Had you been there, the Grays would have taken you both, and the remainder of your lives would have been lived in a torturous and miserable state. There wasn't anything you could have done to help. However, you can help Deltoiga now by helping us. If we do things right and get lucky, the Grays will forget about Deltoiga for a while."

Ursa then says, "I told you it was best to do things on a need-to-know basis. Now you need to know."

Nybo and Ursa leave the room with Major Canis while the others are given an opportunity to join the BLR. Zeta explains to them what it means and what will be expected of them. They unanimously agree. Cindy states that, so long as she can be with Moe, she is in. Joe feels it is the opportunity of a lifetime. Pamuhl is still trying to control her tears as she says, "Let's kill them all!"

CHAPTER 15

I NEVER SIGNED UP FOR THIS

Nybo has spent several weeks with Major Canis, Ursa, and various other spies and double agents. In that period, he has learned the layout of the Grays' underground base that he will soon be entering along with Ursa. The base is one of the major control systems for their underground transport. Nybo has been told that if he can disrupt the system, the Grays will be thrown into total chaos. When that happens, it will delay their plans to take over Earth, and they will pull the Grays from other planets like Deltoiga, creating time to set up a defensive strategy.

Nybo has been learning about the Gray's customs and mannerisms. His ability to change form will allow him to look like a Chinese-Grey human hybrid, a Graynese. These hybrids are the ones mainly used on the control level.

The rest of the group have been training to work in safe houses, learning techniques used for cleansing individuals to clear them of the hypnosis that gives the Grays power over them, as well as how to deactivate the chips that have been inserted into some.

They have also learned how to handle carrier pigeons, which are often utilized by the BLR instead of drones. The Grays' drones will follow the drones sent out by the BLR, sometimes even attack them. With their advanced technology, the Grays have forgotten about old styles of communication. The pigeons are used for about half of the communication between safe houses and BLR bases on Earth.

After two months of preparation, Nybo is ready to infiltrate the Grays' underground base along with Ursa, a human/Gray hybrid. The Grays believe she is working for them. However, she has enough human blood and brain cells remaining that she recognizes the true nasty nature of the Grays. Ursa remained on Earth to infiltrate the BLR, but quickly realized she preferred the BLR over the Grays.

When visiting the Grays' underground base, she has access to level one, the transport system; level two, supplies and maintenance; and level five, the dining and spa area. She does not have access to level three, the human and animal storage area; level four, the experimental laboratory; and level six, the master control level, the level Nybo must enter to temporarily save the world and Deltoiga.

Nybo has an accurate picture of the layout of the laboratory and the master control level from videos he has been viewing. The BLR has created cyborg hybrid mix rabbits, mice, and bats capable of filming through their eyes and relaying the video back to BLR headquarters. The Grays raise rabbits and mice for experimentation. A stray rabbit or mouse, like the ones implemented by the BLR, is not uncommon and is usually ignored. Bats come with the territory.

Ursa and Nybo are ready to begin their mission. There is a vehicle belonging to the Grays that Ursa uses when she is away from the underground base. It is kept hidden a hundred miles from BLR headquarters when she visits. Today, she and Nybo will be dropped off there and use the vehicle to drive to the Grays' underground base.

Nybo says his farewell to the others and takes the form of a Graynese. He is given an identification badge bearing his new name, Dr. Chu. His first name is Au. As Ursa and Dr. Chu are leaving, Major Canis wishes to give them last second instructions and encouragement. He calls out Au Chu, and the others say bless you and gesundheit.

Two and a half hours of driving brings Ursa and Nybo to a cave that they enter. They continue to drive in the cave for an additional twenty minutes. They are met by security guards who recognize Ursa but ask several questions about Dr. Chu. Once convinced he has been ordered to the underground base to perform maintenance on the control level, Nybo and Ursa are cleared and continue driving.

Nybo asks about the air this deep into the cave. Ursa explains that there is an extensive ventilation system that not only provides oxygen but also clears the gas build-up caused by the transport system. A gas called radon is a byproduct of the Grays' fuel mixture. It is forced out of the tunnels and seeps through Earth's surface.

In ten minutes, they arrive at an area for parking that is filled with land-rovers, spacecraft, automobiles, and other types of vehicles, some that Nybo has never seen before. After parking and exiting the car, Nybo and Ursa are met by people wearing white protective suits, shoes, gloves, and head gear with respirator masks. The two newcomers are led to decontamination pods, where they are separated, leaving Nybo, Dr. Chu, alone for the first time.

Nybo removes his clothing and steps into a pod where he is blasted by a shower of foam and water along with something he cannot identify. The pod suddenly swings around and connects with another pod. A door slides open, and after Nybo enters the second pod, it too swings around. A rush of heat hits him just before a strong blast of continuous wind. The pod then swings around connecting with a third pod that is entered by Nybo. After the pod stops turning, Nybo is instructed to stand still. A bright red line of light shoots across the top of the pod and then begins to descend, hitting Nybo and traveling down the entire length of his body, causing him to experience a tickling feeling. He is then instructed to place the forefinger of each hand into a hole on the sides of the pod. A quick zap of energy flows through Nybo's body, and the pod swings around. An announcement is made that decontamination is complete, and a door slides open.

Nybo exits the pod and finds himself standing in a room where he's given a light-blue jumpsuit with his name sewn on the front, along with a white, duster-length lab coat with the name "Dr. Chu" sewn on the left chest.

Exiting the room, Dr. Chu is surrounded by thirty elevators, several escalators, and numerous sets of stairs. Nybo thinks, "They showed me how every level is laid out, where everything is located, but they didn't tell which elevator to take." Ursa enters the room.

Ursa points toward an escalator and says, "Come along. I'll give you a tour of the two top levels. Afterward, you'll be met by one of your coworkers who will show you the lower levels and your primary workstation. I'll meet you at the spa tomorrow at twelve forty-five for a massage."

Ursa steps onto the escalator ahead of Nybo. He looks her over from behind and thinks how interesting she is. He finds he cannot take his eyes off her. Stepping off the escalator onto the transportation level, Ursa says, "I'll show you the two main loading stations, one for passengers and one for cargo."

As Nybo takes a step, Ursa yells, "Watch out!" while pulling him back. Nybo hears a hum and feels a breeze brush past. Ursa says, "Didn't you see the lights? You could have been killed!"

Nybo looks and sees a board with six columns of lights, each with eight rows containing several colors. Ursa explains that the hum and breeze were caused by a transport train. "They move too fast to be seen. You must pay attention to the light board and wait for the proper combination." Nybo thinks how there are a lot of things they did not prepare him for.

Walking along, Ursa says, "Nybo, you will need to act quickly to enter the virus code into the control system. Once it's entered, you will have two to three hours to get out before the system shuts down. I'll be working the parking area to assist the decontamination unit. Once you get out, stand near the car until I get there. You do remember the code for the virus, don't you?"

Nybo feels disappointed by her lack of confidence in him. He gives an inquiring look to Ursa and says, "Do you really think I would be here if I wasn't sure about the code?"

Entering the loading zone, Nybo stops speaking in midsentence.

Ursa looks at him and notices he is staring at a chimpanzee who is loading boxes onto a transportation car. She says, "Oh, you aren't familiar with the humanzees utilized by the Grays. The chimpanzees have been injected with human blood and have had human stem cells fused into their brains. They work throughout the base. The more advanced ones can speak and communicate telepathically. They work in the lower levels. Some are used as servants in the spa and dining pool."

Nybo does not bother to ask about the term *dining pool*, something he'll soon regret.

Descending to the supply and maintenance level, they head toward a conference room. Nybo is impressed by the diligence and efficiency of the *humanzees* as they work in unison at a high pace. Entering the conference room, Ursa introduces Dr. Chu to his coworker, Dr. Mai. A long table is surrounded by various Graynese department heads, who welcome Dr. Chu.

"The meeting is just wrapping up. Dr. Chu, please sit and join us," says Dr. Mai. "What was your first name?"

After Dr. Chu replies, Dr. Mai repeats, "Au Chu," which draws a response of gesundheit from the others.

Just as the meeting is about to end, Dr. Ping, who is sitting at the left end of the table, initiates a conversation with his rival, Dr. Pong, who is seated at the right end of the table. They disagree on something, and the conversation gets a little heated as they begin to argue. Dr. Ping speaks and all heads turn to the left. Dr. Pong responds and all heads turn to the right. Then Ping refutes and heads turn left. Pong makes a quick comeback and heads turn right. Then Ping, heads left, then Pong, heads right. The pace quickens, Ping, Pong, Ping, Pong, heads turning left, right, left, right. Finally, Dr. Nett gets in the middle and disrupts the volley, declaring it a draw. All the others stand and clap.

The meeting ends, and Ursa says goodbye to Dr. Chu, reminding him of their massage appointment scheduled for the next day. Dr. Mai says, "Come on, I'll give you a tour of the other levels on the way to our workstation. By the way, before I forget, you have a lunch appointment today with the big boss, Dr. Ding-Bang. His first name is Da, but never call him that if you're interested in keeping your job. He hates it."

Dr. Chu repeats, "Dr. Da Ding-Bang."

The two Graynese doctors enter the third level, which shocks Dr. Chu, causing him to exclaim, "Oh!"

Dr. Mai asks," What?"

Dr. Chu looks at him and asks, "What?"

Dr. Mai explains, "You said, 'Oh.' That's my name, Oh. I'm Oh Mai Au Chu." Others on the level respond with gesundheit. Dr. Chu relates how overwhelmed he is at the number of humans and animals being stored.

Dr. Mai introduces Dr. Chu to Dr. Woo, who is the head of the storage level. Dr. Woo says, "Nice to meet you, Dr. Chu. I'm Woo with o."

Dr. Mai asks, What?"

Dr. Woo responds, "Not you oh, Woo o. I show you around."

They see seemingly endless, large, glass tubes filled with an indescribable color of liquid, each containing some type of animal or human. Several contain strange combinations from past experiments of one animal crossed with another or a human crossed with an animal. There are humans with eight arms, and rabbits with human ears. Others are filled with human or animal organs.

The vessels are stacked one upon another and line the walls as far as Dr. Chu can see. They walk by a door labeled with a danger sign. Dr. Woo tells Dr. Chu the door opens to the frozen storage area. Dr. Woo warns, "If you do not dress coweckree, you fweeze in there. Then you become experiment." Dr. Chu and Dr. Mai enter an elevator and descend to the fourth level.

Entering the fourth level, Dr. Chu and Dr. Mai are greeted by another Graynese doctor. Dr. Mai says, "Dr. Wu, meet Au Chu."

"Gesundheit," responds Dr. Wu while turning toward Dr. Chu and asking, "And what's your name?"

"Au Chu," responds Nybo.

"Gesundheit," says Dr. Wu. "I'm Wu, no o."

"What?" asks Dr. Mai.

"Not you oh, Wu no o."

"Oh," replies Dr. Chu.

Dr. Wu groans and says, "No o, u, ah, never mind. I might have something to help with your colds."

Touring the experimental lab makes Dr. Chu feel ill. He struggles to stay focused and tries not to turn pale from all the organs and body parts strewn about. They stop to see what Dr. Wee is working on when someone calls out, "Wu, Wee, come see."

Moving to the workstation, they find a centipede barking like a dog. They are told to watch while the centipede rolls over on command. There is also a dog with eight legs and a head on each end.

As the tour continues, there's strange experiment after strange experiment. Some are interesting some are grotesque, like jars containing human heads with eyes on the front and back. Near the end of the lab, the air becomes increasingly odorous. A door labeled Waste is opened by Dr. Wu, and the odor becomes unbearable. Dr. Chu can no longer stand it. The only way he can stay is by reminding himself that he is saving Deltoiga and his human friends on Earth.

There are different disposal stations in the room. Some are labeled Good, where the best quality items like livers and hearts are disposed down a chute, along with arms and legs. Another is labeled midgrade where lesser quality organs and body parts are disposed. The final station is labeled ocean. Where garbage and useless organs and body parts are flushed out into the ocean. Human, animal, and alien organs and parts are blended and disposed of.

Moving on to the control center, the doctors are met by Dr. Bingwen Wang, the lead doctor. Dr. Wang says, "You must be Au Chu." Gesundheit can be heard throughout the room.

Dr. Wang asks Dr. Chu several questions about the control system and the maintenance program. While Dr. Chu answers, he hears Dr. Wang say, "You wrong."

Dr. Chu freezes and asks, "What?"

Dr. Wang points and says, "That's Dr. Yu Rong over there. He's been away for a couple of days."

"Oh," says Dr. Chu.

"What," asks Dr. Mai.

CHAPTER 16

HAVE TO EAT AND RUN

Dr. Oh Mai shows Dr. Au Chu around the control center. Hidden in a corner is one of the BLR cyborg rabbits. The rabbit is sending video to BLR headquarters where the others see Nybo and start cheering. "It's nice to know he's made it this far," says Major Canis.

Dr. Chu arrives at his workstation, relieved to see the equipment is what he was expecting. Dr. Mai says, "Don't get too involved, Doctor. You have lunch in five minutes. You don't want to keep Ding-Bang waiting. You recall how to get there."

Dr. Chu replies, "Yes, elevator fourteen."

"Right you are, Chu. When you enter the dining area, you will be met by a humanzee who will assist you.

Dr. Chu exits elevator fourteen, and is greeted by a talking humanzee. The humanzee says, "Welcome, Dr. Chu, you will be dining in Dr. Ding-Bang's private pool. Please follow me."

While walking to Dr. Ding-Bang's pool, Nybo thinks how odd it is to eat in a swimming pool. He decides it could be relaxing. The humanzee gives Dr. Chu a swimsuit and leads him to a changing room. Dr. Chu is told that, once suited, he can use the door at the other end of the dressing room to enter the pool area.

After showering, Dr. Chu enters the pool area. Dr. Ding-Bang has not arrived yet. A sudden stench rushes up Dr. Chu's nose. As he looks in the pool, he sees blood-colored water with human and animal organs circulating around, along with arms, legs and heads. There is a splash as a human liver comes flying down a chute into the pool. It turns out the waste chute from the lab labeled "Good" dumps into various dining pools. Dr. Chu cannot take it and finds an urn on a table. Removing the lid from the urn, Dr. Chu vomits into it. Replacing the lid, Dr. Chu realizes that, to save Deltoiga, he must endure whatever is about to happen.

Dr. Ding-Bang enters the pool area and welcomes Dr. Chu. Looking into the urn, he says, "Ah, how splendid, tapioca for dessert. Let's plunge into lunch, shall we?"

They sit down in the pool, and Dr. Chu feels a cow heart bounce off his leg. There is a splash under the waste chute as another liver is dumped into the pool. Dr. Ding-Bang says, "Umm, fresh liver, one of my favorites."

The Grays do not have stomachs or colons, so they absorb nutrients through their skin. That is the reason for the dining pool and massages.

Dr. Da Ding-Bang asks Dr. Chu several questions about the system maintenance and about some new programs the Grays are about to launch. A human head appears to be looking at them as it floats by. Dr. Chu answers most of the questions but admits to a lack of knowledge on one of the new programs. Recognizing Dr. Ding-Bang's suspicious look, Dr. Chu explains he was about to begin the training for that program when he was called upon to perform maintenance at this base.

Dr. Ding-Bang is satisfied with Dr. Chu's response and, brushing away a pig's head, says, "Let me know when you are full doctor."

Dr. Chu responds, "I've had more than my fill already."

"Well, let's head into the spa then," says Dr. Ding-Bang as a human arm splashes into the pool. Grabbing the urn off the table, Dr. Ding-Bang walks to a door that leads to the spa room. The spa room is surrounded by doors connected to other pools and is filled with massage tables.

The two doctors lay on adjacent tables and are tended to by humanzees. The humanzees dip their hands into the urn and begin massaging the doctors. Dr. Chu senses that he must appear green as he fights the urge to vomit while being massaged with his own. The humanzees continue to dip and rub. Dr. Ding-Bang inquiries about the flavor of the tapioca. Both humanzees respond that they have never smelt or felt this flavor before.

After what seems an eternity, the massages end. Dr. Chu thanks Dr. Ding-Bang who says, "We must do this again soon. How about Friday?"

Dr. Chu says, "Yes, Friday," while thinking that he must complete his mission before then. Dr. Chu takes the best shower of his life, and although he scrubs himself several times, he is unable to eliminate the odor. Still feeling weak and lightheaded, Dr. Chu returns to his work area.

Settling into his workstation, Dr. Chu finds several interesting things, including a transport bus pilot manual. Scanning through the manual, he is amazed by the advanced technology and decides it would be challenging to try and operate a transportation bus. It would be nothing like flying a Deltoigan spacecraft.

Dr. Chu sees moneymaking projects that are currently being worked on, which are to be given to American companies run by human hybrids controlled by the Grays. The money raised will go to fund the Grays' Earth projects. There are things like tires that never go flat and last for up to three-hundred-thousand miles, often exceeding the life of the vehicles they're placed on; small windmills located on the grills of electric cars to charge the battery while driving; golf balls with GPS; and gardening seeds which grow to maturity in four days.

The following day, Dr. Chu navigates his way through various programs including the transport control program. Just as he is devising a scheme on how and when to implement the virus, he is reminded of his massage appointment. Reluctantly, he heads to the elevator. Every instinct in his body tells him not to go, but he must meet Ursa. He feels a little excited about meeting her.

Entering the spa room, Dr. Chu finds Ursa lying on a massage table. "There you are," says Ursa, "I was afraid you had forgotten."

"I wish I could have forgotten," responds the doctor.

Ursa asks, "How are things going?"

Looking around the room before responding, Dr. Chu says, "I have it figured out. I can make it happen by this afternoon."

Ursa replies, "That's great, but it would be better if you wait till tomorrow."

Dr. Chu asks, "What do you mean? I thought you wanted to get this done. I just want to get it over with and get out of here."

A pair of humanzees enter the room, each carrying a gallon-size can. The conversation is put on hold until they can be alone. The humanzees dip their hands into the cans and begin rubbing pig lard over the bodies of Ursa and Dr. Chu. One of the humanzees asks, "Is this satisfactory, sir?"

Dr. Chu replies, "Yes. This is a nice change of pace after yesterday's massage."

After a forty-minute lard rub down, the humanzees leave the room. Ursa tells Dr. Chu, "Tomorrow morning around eleven o'clock, finish installing the virus. It will be lunchtime then. You can tell the others that you need to go to the lab before lunch to take care of a programming issue. Head up to the parking area. I'll be watching for you."

A humanzee enters the room with fresh towels and informs them that their allotted time is over. Ursa and Dr. Chu leave the spa in opposite directions.

Dr. Chu spends the night wide-awake, thinking about getting the mission done. He is more on edge than he was the night that he and Joe escaped from the hospital. If anything goes wrong, it could not only cost him his life but also mean the end of Deltoiga, Ursa, his other Earth friends, and Earth itself. Staying cool and acting normal is the only chance for success.

In the morning while Dr. Chu is walking to the control center, Dr. Da Ding-Bang spots him and calls out, "Au Chu." Gesundheit can be heard throughout the area. Dr. Ding-Bang asks, "How about lunch? Shall we say at ten fifty?"

Dr. Chu asks himself how to get out of this one. Dr. Da Ding-Bang expects things to go as he plans and does not do well with refusals. Dr. Chu thinks, *If I accept, the mission is delayed, not to mention sitting in that pool again. I must somehow get him to change the time. He'll not accept my work schedule as a reason to decline.* Thinking quickly Dr. Chu says, "Wonderful! Although the word from the lab is that they'll be dumping fresh livers at eleven thirty."

"Hmm," responds Dr. Ding-Bang. "Eleven thirty, it is then."

It is almost eleven. Dr. Oh Mai has been gabbing away all morning. Dr. Chu must finally ask Dr. Mai to give him time to work on a project that must be completed ASAP. Dr. Mai reluctantly returns to his own work area. Dr. Chu, while constantly looking over his shoulders, installs the virus code.

After a couple of minutes, he heads for the elevators. "Where are you going?" asks Dr. Mai. "It's a little early for lunch."

Dr. Chu replies, "I must head up to the experimental lab to explain the new system to the scientists."

Dr. Mai becomes suspicious. How can Dr. Chu go to the experimental lab for a meeting and make it to the dining level by eleven thirty? People have changed vacation plans to dine with Dr. Ding-Bang. Nobody would ever keep him waiting for a meeting.

Dr. Mai waits for Dr. Chu's elevator door to shut and monitors the floors being traveled. Seeing the elevator go all the way to the decontamination level, Dr. Mai takes an elevator there. As the elevator door slides open, he is met by two decontamination workers. Seeing Dr. Chu entering a decontamination pod, Dr. Mai excitedly calls out, "Au Chu!" The workers say gesundheit. As the pod door is sliding shut, Dr. Mai again calls out, "Au Chu!"

One of the decontamination workers demands, "Would you please cover your sneezes! I'm afraid you're not going anywhere with that cold."

Dr. Mai notices that Dr. Chu has cleared decontamination and is entering the parking area. Dr. Mai says, "Damn you, Au Chu!" and insists that he must be allowed to skip the decontamination process and be allowed to go directly to the parking area.

The workers inform him, "You're not going anywhere, and since you refuse to cover your sneezes, you will be quarantined for a couple of days."

Dr. Mai frantically states, "Don't you see? Au Chu is out there!"

One of the workers says, "That's it. We're calling security."

Dr. Mai replies," Yes, call them. Call them."

As Dr. Chu begins to walk across the parking area, he is spotted by Ursa, who approaches him and begins speaking. They walk by a transportation bus as it is parking, and Dr. Chu freezes. He can see that it is full of Deltoigans. Albie III did not believe Nybo when he had warned him about the Grays.

Ursa asks what is wrong, and Dr. Chu says, "Those are all Deltoigans. I can't just leave them."

The transport bus door opens, and as the crew exits, Ursa says to them, "My gosh! Didn't you get the warning? These people are all infected. You weren't supposed to bring them here. You are all infected now! Hurry! Hurry. Get to decontamination. Afterward, you'll be quarantined."

The crew hurries to decontamination. Dr. Chu and Ursa usher the Deltoigans out of the bus and squeeze them into Ursa's vehicle. Security enters the parking area as Ursa drives away. "This isn't going the smoothest," she says, "We still have a checkpoint to clear. I don't know how we can do it with all these Deltoigans."

Security is still trying to decipher exactly what is happening as Ursa nears the checkpoint. Dr. Chu changes to his natural Deltoigan form. The other Deltoigans are awed. "Hey, you're Nybo, the voyager!"

Nybo responds, "That's right. Listen! You all must act now! Change form into an animal of some sort. There's no time to explain. Just do it! Your lives and Deltoiga's survival depend on it. Change *now*!"

There are six Deltoigan visitors in the vehicle; four of them change to an animal form just as they reach the checkpoint. Nybo changes back to Dr. Chu. The checkpoint guards ask, "What's this now? We aren't aware of you all leaving the base."

Dr. Chu states, "I'm doing some atmospheric test with some of the prototypes. If things work as expected, we'll soon own the world."

After a little further discussion, the vehicle exits the checkpoint. The guards watch the vehicle drive away as a security bulletin requesting a lockdown appears. No vehicles may arrive or depart. The guards yell for the vehicle to stop, but they are too late.

CHAPTER 17

WHAT ARE WE DOING NOW?

Usra, Nybo, and the others arrive at BLR headquarters and are given a hero's reception. The vehicle is driven away, headed south to Los Angles, hoping to create a diversion. Nybo is relieved to change back to human form.

The Deltoigans are confused and uncertain about Nybo. They still believe the Grays are a kind and generous race that only wish to help their planet and people.

While the Deltoigans are eating spaghetti, Nybo and Ursa try to explain what is happening and who the Grays really are. Both Nybo and Ursa are called away for a debriefing.

The Deltoigans talk among themselves and find that their numbers are split on who to believe, Nybo or the Grays.

Pamuhl enters the room and changes to her Deltoigan form. The other Deltoigans had all heard of Pamuhl, but none had ever met her. They are relieved and surprised to see another Deltoigan. After telling her story to the others, the atmosphere in the room becomes much calmer.

The evening is spent with tales from Deltoiga. Nybo and Pamuhl are delighted to hear about old friends and familiar places.

Everyone at BLR headquarters is anxious to learn about the effects of the virus Nybo has installed. Video from the cyborg rabbits and mice show a sudden commotion in the control room of the Grays' base. The transport system has been disrupted. All the transportation vehicles are stopped. There are a few reported crashes and rumors of important Gray leaders dying.

Pandemonium erupts in the control room. Cheers echo throughout BLR headquarters. A celebration goes well into the night. As Nybo and Major Canis speak to one another, Nybo asks, "What now?"

The following day, a meeting is held to review options on moving forward. Nybo insist that Pamuhl be allowed to return to Deltoiga. He can easily instruct her on how to operate his spacecraft. There have been several changes to Deltoigan spacecraft since the Albie. Nybo is sure Pamuhl is smart enough to understand how to operate a modern spacecraft. He can teach her with one easy lesson.

Despite the risk of going into space while the Grays are humming around like mad hornets, Deltoiga must be warned about the true nature of the Grays. It is likely that a small spacecraft could go unnoticed with the Grays' attention focused on Earth and Betelgeuse.

Things are going to get tough. The Grays will be arriving by the busload. They will do all they can to get to the bottom of who is responsible for what happened to their transport system. The BLR will not be able to move so freely for a while.

It is agreed that Pamuhl will return to Deltoiga. The eldest of the Deltoigans now on Earth, Fraxel, will go with her to verify the peril of believing the Grays. In time, a Deltoigan space bus can come to Earth for Nybo and the others. Meanwhile, Nybo can care for them. The newly arrived Deltoigans are confused, and their heads are reeling.

Moe, Joe, and Cindy will leave tomorrow for a safe house they will work at. Moe is excited to find out that he will be getting his Camaro back. "One thing," says Major Canis, "your car no longer has any slogans on it."

"Thank goodness," replies Moe.

Major Canis continues by saying, "It's a good time to tell you that your car is no longer white. Way too risky to leave it the original color."

Moe responds, "Not white?"

Major Canis says, "We had to go with the color least appealing to the Grays. Pink."

"What?" responds Moe, "I have a pink car!"

The others laugh. "Once you go gay, you are there to stay," Joe says jokingly.

On Deltoiga, the Grays' ambassador, Will Robinson, addresses the Wisdom Core. Will Robinson was a human who was lost in space. He was abducted by the Grays and, as the result of strange experiments, has evolved into a half Gray, half human, who now works for the Grays. Will Robinson informs the Wisdom Core, "I'm afraid some important business has come up. We'll be leaving right away. Do not fear. We'll return when a certain situation has been resolved and those who were responsible have been eradicated—those pesky Earthlings. They're trying to take over all planets and peoples. They will find their way to Deltoiga eventually if we don't stop them. Deltoiga could be in danger."

One of the Wisdom Core responds, "Danger, Will Robinson?"

The following day on Earth, the group tearfully exchanges goodbyes. Pamuhl and Fraxel will soon be leaving for Nybo's spacecraft. They will be escorted by Zeta, who feels it is too risky. Following Nybo's directions and using her jomo, Pamuhl should have no problem finding the spacecraft. Flying it is the concern.

Moe, Joe, and Cindy climb into the Camaro. Nybo tells Moe, "You look good in pink. It really fits you."

After a sad, nervous laugh, Zeta instructs them, "Go directly to the safe house. Get there as quickly as possible. Be very cautious and trust no one. The Grays will be diligently searching for BLR members."

The vehicle begins moving, and waves are exchanged until the Camaro is out of sight. They have been assigned to a safe house in Minneapolis where strange things are happening, too close to the Canadian border.

The BLR intelligence has learned that there is a possibility they have located Jous. He is believed to be a park ranger in the Midwest. Nybo and the other Deltoigans are going to investigate.

It is also possible that Ef is a television preacher in Florida, but that has not been confirmed. Nybo sticks with his human form. The other Deltoigans must take a human form, so they now appear as a group of nuns. The evening prior, they had watched television for the first time and seen a documentary on Mother Teresa. Ursa, who is now being sought by the Grays, will be the driver. She and Nybo have been developing a strong bond.

Zeta warns Pamuhl about traveling south to Arizona. "You realize this is crazy. We are taking a great risk going to the spacecraft, which we don't even know we'll find. If we do find it, and if you are able to fly it, you will be detected by the Grays. The question is whether they will bother to abduct a small random spacecraft. Their focus will be totally on Earth, which doesn't have rockets or shuttles that look anything like your spacecraft. If you are caught, Pamhul, and now you also, Fraxel, you will never be heard from again. There won't be any hope of being rescued."

Pamuhl replies, "None of that matters. I've got to get to Deltoiga and convince them of the danger they're in. If I fail, I accept the consequences. At least I know I did what I could. You would do the same thing if it were your planet." Zeta nods his head in agreement.

INTERMISSION

CHAPTER 18

MOE, JOE, AND CINDY

It is the second day since the disruption of the Grays' underground transportation system. The group of heroes split up and go their separate ways. Ursa is in the most danger since the Grays know her and can identify her. If she is caught, she will be given the most torturous treatment anyone can receive for as long as she can endure it. Death will be her only comfort.

Pamuhl, Zeta, and Fraxel are traveling south to Arizona, headed into a hotbed of angry Grays. The journey places them in great peril, but driving a car decorated with gay slogans might help. If not, the outcome will be ugly.

Driving for hours with little communication between them, Moe, Joe, and Cindy approach South Dakota. They are feeling a little nervous and a lot scared. Being separated from the others has caused them to feel insecure. Moe says, "I hope this pink paint job works."

Joe responds, "Wow, I never thought I would hear you say something like that." After a couple of quiet moments, Joe observes, "It sure is boring traveling without Nybo. I really miss the little guy." As they approach a diner, they decide to stop and eat.

Throughout the meal, they talk about their new assignment. None of them has ever been to Minneapolis before. The waitress brings the tab and observes that it looks like it could rain at any moment. The sky is very dark.

Four tall men wearing thick, dark sunglasses, trench coats, and fedoras enter the diner. Cindy states, "That's weird. Who would wear dark glasses on a day like today?"

Joe agrees. "Yeah, who would wear dark glasses on a day like today, unless they're—" He stops in midsentence, and the three of them look at each other with wide eyes. Joe finishes his sentence. "Grays."

The Grays' transportation system is down, so they now drive cars. Every available agent is combing the country, looking for Ursa, Dr. Chu, and BLR members. An army of Grays are headed to Earth. They are coming from Betelgeuse and Rigel but will soon be followed by other star systems.

Their intention is to first eliminate the BLR and then devastate Earth by killing half the population and enslaving the rest. The plan is to harvest the natural resources and send them to Gray bases in outer space. Once the resources have been depleted, they will torture and execute the slaves. The most useful will be spared and sent to work camps on other planets. Earth will be blown to pieces, becoming nothing more than a meteorite shower.

The four men are seated across the diner. Moe, Joe, and Cindy begin to panic. Leaving the money for the tab on the table, they head for the door. The four Grays sense the fear being experienced by the trio and suddenly turn in unison to look at them. As the group exits the diner, one of the Grays states, "There's something odd about those people." He then walks over to the door and observes the trio getting into the car. As he returns to the table he says, "What an ugly car. I wouldn't be caught dead in a car like that."

Driving away from the diner, Moe continuously checks the rearview mirror. After a few miles, he says, "I don't think they're following us."

Cindy says, "Zeta said we were all in danger. Now, I believe him."

Joe says, "Yeah, let's just get to Minneapolis. I'm not going to feel safe until we're standing in the safe house."

Moe agrees saying, "Ditto. Only we need to stop for gas soon."

Twenty miles down the road is a gas station. A vehicle, which can best be described as a hippy van, has just left there en route to the Storm Area 51 event. There are several young people dressed in alien costumes riding in the van. Within a mile, the van is filled with a cloud of marijuana smoke.

Back at the gas station, a woman wearing a golden jumpsuit emerges from the restroom. The jumpsuit gives her an alien appearance, especially since she is wearing a headband with antennas. Her name is Star. To her horror, she has been forgotten by the group in the van. She now is standing outside of the gas station in the middle of nowhere. Half angry and half frightened, she fights back tears while she looks around.

Twenty minutes pass, and Moe, Joe and Cindy pull into the gas station. Cindy goes to the ladies' room, which is accessed from outside. While Moe is putting gas in the car, Joe, who is wearing his Area 51 T-shirt, enters the station. While grabbing some chips and drinks, he looks up and sees Star. It is love at first sight.

Joe can hardly form words but manages to say, "I really like your outfit."

While Star is saying thank you, she notices Joe's shirt and asks, "Are you going to Storm Area 51?"

Joe has been so busy dealing with aliens lately he has not even heard of the event. After Star explains it to him, she tells him about how she is stranded. A heavy rain begins to fall.

Joe thinks that he cannot invite her to go with them, but she is too beautiful to not offer help. *Zeta never actually said we couldn't bring a guest.* He tells her, "My friends and I are going to Minneapolis. I know it's the wrong way, but you're welcome to come with us."

Star replies, "That would be great, though I'm not really dressed for that."

"You might be surprised," responds Joe.

Moe has gone to the restroom, and Cindy is in the store. When they return to the car, Joe and Star are sitting in the back seat. Neither of them notices Star. As Moe pulls out onto the road, he takes a swig of water and checks the rearview mirror for Grays. He is startled when he sees Star and swallows down the wrong pipe, causing him to cough and spit water onto the windshield and dashboard. Cindy assumes there must be Grays behind them and turns to look. She screams and audibly passes gas when she sees Star.

Joe says, "Oh good, you guys have met Star."

Moe excitedly asks, "What are you thinking? Why is she here?"

Star replies, "I was stranded, so Joe invited me to ride along with you guys."

Moe sternly says, "I wasn't talking to you. And why are you dressed like an alien?"

Joe replies, "She was on her way to Storm Area 51."

Moe again states, "I wasn't talking to you."

The car stops half on the road and half on the shoulder. Moe turns to face them and states, "You know this isn't acceptable. It might be the dumbest thing you've ever done."

Star volunteers to leave. Joe says, "I know nobody was expecting this, but no one ever said we couldn't have a guest."

Cindy chimes in, "I don't believe anybody felt they had to say it. It's hard to imagine anyone would be that naïve; to involve a stranger. Well she might as well come along now, if anyone has seen her in our car, she's in as much peril as we are."

Star states, "Okay, this is where I get off. What's wrong with you people? It's like you should be committed or something." Both Moe and Joe chuckle.

Joe says, "Look, guys, I really like Star. We can't leave her out in the rain. I bet Zeta would do the same thing."

Moe says, "I can hear him now. 'Why must you people insist on drawing attention to yourselves?' Ugh, let's just get going."

Cindy says, "Well, at least she's dressed for it." Star gives Joe a confused look.

Joe tells her, "We have lots to talk about on the way."

As they drive down the road, Joe is trying to figure out what to tell Star. How does he explain to her what is going on? How much can and should he tell her? Traffic is stopped ahead. They are no longer moving.

An officer approaches each car along the line, explaining that it will be a while. He approaches the Camaro, and Moe lowers the window. The officer says, "Good afternoon, folks, I've never seen a pink Camaro before. You guys all gay?"

Moe replies, "Hey, we're not gay. What's going on?"

The officer tells them, "It's really ugly up there. Two guys in a pickup truck had worked on their brakes this morning.

They were drinking heavily and forgot to reattach the brake line. They went out to get more beer, and when they went down the hill, they couldn't stop. They made it down and then up the next hill. They bought more beer and figured since they had made it there, they could make it back. Going down the hill, they were close to one hundred miles per hour, and the driver lost control. He was thrown from the vehicle, but his buddy took a plunge down the mountainside. Not much left of him. It'll be another twenty to thirty minutes before traffic will move again."

Waiting on traffic is making Moe edgy. He constantly checks the mirror for Grays. "At least, we have chips and drinks," says Joe.

Star begins asking questions about the nature of their trip. Suddenly, Moe blurts out, "Oh crap."

A car driven by the Grays from the restaurant stops behind them. "What is it? What's going on?" asks Star.

Moe says, "Stay calm, everyone. There's nothing we can do right now."

"What is it?" repeats Star.

Joe asks her, "Eh, do you believe in aliens?"

Star replies, "Come on, I'm not that naïve. I have never seen a UFO or an alien or a ghost. I was just going to Storm Area 51 for the parties."

Joe begins to explain things by saying, "It's kind of a long story."

Moe butts in, "Joe, this isn't a good time for that story. We're all remaining calm—remember? Besides, we should talk abou—oh crap, one of them is coming!"

One of the men from the diner approaches the car. Moe puts down the window and can hardly contain his fear. He has a sick feeling and begins to salivate under his tongue, feeling as though he could vomit.

The man with the dark glasses says, "You guys were at the diner. Do you know what's going on?"

Moe tells him about what the officer had said. The man says thank you and states, "Man, you have an ugly car, you should really get a new one."

"We're gay," blurts out Cindy, causing the man to take a step back. Moe moans.

The man asks, "Hey, you guys haven't seen a tall skinny lady with a short fat man, have you? He goes by Dr. Au Chu."

Star says, "Gesundheit."

Moe answers, "No. Other than cars going by, you are the only people we've seen."

The man thanks them again and asks, "Where you guys headed?"

Moe is trying to think of an answer when he hears Star say, "Minneapolis."

Moe's heart sinks. The man says, "We were thinking about heading there ourselves. We have several friends coming to that area. You might say friends from out of town. From faraway places." The man looks at Star and asks, "What planet are you from?"

Star replies, "Men are from Mars; women are from Venus."

The man gives her an inquisitive look and says, "I've been to Venus. There are no women there. There are only Venusians, who are about three feet tall and live underground. They're hermaphrodites." The man's attitude has changed to a more suspicious, aggressive nature.

Joe quickly blurts out, "It's just a costume. She's not really an alien."

The man's eyebrows rise above the dark glasses. He looks over everybody in the vehicle before stepping back. Moe states, "Oh good. Traffic is starting to move again."

The man has a stern look on his face as he tells Star, "It isn't very smart to pretend to be something you are not. You can get into a lot of trouble that way. People get exterminated."

Star becomes very uncomfortable and squirms in her seat. The man says, "Well, have a good trip," and returns to his car.

The pink Camaro gets underway. Star is restless, confused, and becoming angry. "All right, what's going on here!" she demands to know.

Cindy laughs and says, "Baby, you are on the trip of a lifetime. You're all in now."

Moe says, "Now would be a good time for that long story. She may as well know everything now that they've identified her with us. If we go down, she's going down with us."

Joe begins the story with a nervous, "Ha-ha, uh, you're not going to believe this."

The story goes on for hours, with lots of interruptions and questions. The skies clear as night falls. There is what appears to be a heavy meteorite shower to the north. The reality is it is raining UFOs.

Star continues to ask questions. Meteorites continue falling into the dawn. The Camaro continues its journey, with the occupants unaware there is now a drone hovering above them. The Grays from the diner got suspicious of them after the traffic stop and reported the group. They are now driving under the radar.

CHAPTER 19

IT'S A LONG WAY TO ARIZONA

Pamuhl, Zeta, and Fraxel

Zeta is driving as the trio heads south. Fraxel is asking question after question about Earth. Pamuhl feels distracted by the questions as she is full of adrenalin and concern about finding and flying the spacecraft.

Zeta is trying to decide the best route for avoiding encounters with the Grays. He is not coming up with good options. He takes one last stab at trying to talk Pamuhl into postponing the trip and allowing time for things to blow over. Not a chance.

Zeta states, "If they catch us, do yourself a favor and don't get taken alive. They're masters at torture. During World War II before Hitler went off the deep end, there were several Grays who were prominent Nazi officers. They were constantly conducting experiments on prisoners of war, not just the Jews. To this day, there are still Nazi war criminals who have never been found; that's because most of them are Grays who are no longer on Earth."

Pamuhl asks, "What kind of experiments?"

Zeta states, "Most were torture experiments to see what Earthlings are capable of handling. For example, at the concentration camps, a random Jew would be forced to remove his clothing and stand outside naked in subzero weather. Realize that Jews in these camps were malnourished and barely had an ounce of meat on their bones. If they survived through the night, cold water was dumped on them several times the next day until death occurred."

"Sorry I asked," says Pamuhl.

Zeta continues. "The Grays were impressed by the way the German citizens were so easily indoctrinated. An entire nation taught to be jealous of a race because of their success. When a nation becomes jealous, hatred is quick to follow. It's amazing what one human is capable of doing to another."

The drive remains quiet for several minutes until Fraxel asks the umpteenth question, which tests Pamuhl's patience. She takes a deep breath and turns on the radio. "Hey, here's something they do on Earth. Listen to this for a while." Other than the sound of the radio, the vehicle remains quiet, allowing Zeta and Pamuhl to focus on their concerns.

The news comes on the radio, and the weatherman announces there will be clear skies. "Perfect conditions for viewing the stars. Maybe we'll have another unexpected meteorite shower like the one last night."

Pamuhl notices a change of expression on Zeta's face. "What is it?" she asks.

Zeta looks at her. "We only hope that was an unexpected meteorite shower. If those were spacecraft belonging to the Grays, oh my."

"What?" asks Pamuhl.

Zeta responds with concern, "We were expecting retaliation after the transport attack; but if they're bringing in an army, oh my, this could be much bigger than we were planning on."

As evening approaches, Zeta says, "Okay, guys, we'll stop for gas and dinner, then no more stops till I drop you off at the spacecraft. Where should we eat?"

Pamuhl immediately answers, "Italian." She tells Fraxel that while on Earth, he must try spaghetti. "Aside from Cindy and *Wheel of Fortune*, that's what I'll miss most about this place."

They are in luck and come across an Italian restaurant. All you can eat spaghetti night. It does not take long for Zeta to be full. He is anxious, and wants to get going. Pamuhl tells him they are just getting started.

An undeclared race develops between Fraxel and Pamuhl to see who can eat the most the fastest. After their fifth serving, they are informed that management has cut them off.

After eating, they stop for gas, and Fraxel is introduced to coffee. He drinks it and states, "Wow, when it comes to food, Earth is like dining in Good Haven."

Night has fallen, and there is another unexpected meteorite shower. Zeta is concerned but feels oddly relieved. It is obvious to him that there is about to be big trouble on Earth. But with all the spacecraft that are arriving, it might be safer for traveling. The Grays already on Earth will be busy receiving the ones arriving and not out searching for BLR members.

With the chaos in the sky, there is a better chance of Pamuhl and Fraxel slipping their spacecraft through unnoticed.

A passenger on one of the unexpected meteorites is Will Robinson. He has been informed that he is no longer an ambassador. He is now being sent to Earth to hunt the BLR. The leadership of the Grays want to wipe out the BLR on Earth before they proceed with the takeover plan. They do not want to fight both the Earthlings and the BLR at the same time. Once the BLR have been eliminated, the humans will be a breeze.

Pamuhl asks Zeta, "Do you need to warn someone about this?"

Zeta replies, "The BLR already know. The Grays can hardly make a move we don't know about. A large majority of the double agents and spies end up working for the BLR. The thing about the Grays is that first they alienate you, and then they alienate you. That is why most of the double agents and spies defect to the BLR."

Pamuhl states, "I don't think I understand the alienate parts."

"Let me explain," states Zeta. "First, they abduct Earthlings, people and creatures from other planets, and, through genetic experimentation, turn them into aliens. Thus, they alienate them. Then they treat them poorly and push them away, alienating them."

They drive through the night, undetected by Grays. The sky is a light show.

Entering the desert, the vehicle is suddenly being tracked by a drone. Following Nybo's directions and utilizing Pamuhl's jomo, they manage to drive within two miles of the spacecraft, where the terrain makes further automobile travel impossible. "Looks like we walk from here," says Zeta.

Pamuhl points southeast and says, "This way." They begin the trek. The drone is hovering a short distance behind them.

They walk at a rapid pace. Pamuhl is focusing on her jomo and leading the way. Zeta is concerned about the drone and stops as he is suddenly overtaken by an eerie feeling.

"Why are we stopping?" asks Pamuhl.

Two very tall, lizard-like men appear from out of nowhere. They point weapons at the trio. One of them says, "Hey, that's the one they call Pamuhl, from the cold-case system."

The other says, "Yes, we'll get a nice reward for this. We don't need all of them, so let's take her and eliminate the others."

As they raise their weapons, Zeta reaches under his shirt and produces a chi-scattering CS5000-model ray gun and shoots one of them. Instantly losing consciousness, the shot Gray falls to the ground, bouncing off the other Gray on the way down. The impact forces the other Gray's weapon to move at the very moment it is being fired. The shot intended for Zeta hits Fraxel, reducing him to a pile of ashes on the ground.

Zeta shoots and hits the second Gray. Within seconds, the Grays vanish. Only their weapons remain lying on the ground. The drone hovers above.

The CS5000 causes the bodies bioelectricity to instantly increase to a rapid flow, causing the victim to lose consciousness. The bioelectricity then increases to an extreme temperature. Within seconds, the victim's body disappears.

Pamuhl states, "My God, Fraxel!"

Zeta tells her, "Pamuhl, we must hurry.

"Can't we build some type of monument for him," asks Pamuhl

Zeta urgently replies, "There is no time. They are on to us. Let's get you to the spacecraft."

They continue to the spacecraft, their pace dictated by Pamuhl's jomo. She stops and says, "There it is!"

Zeta cannot see anything. He asks, "Pamuhl, without Fraxel, there's nobody to back up your story. They wouldn't believe Nybo when he tried to warn them. Do you still think it's wise for you to go?"

Pamuhl responds by giving him a look of disbelief. She then notices a cloud of dust rapidly approaching. She points. "Baby, there's no other choice."

Zeta turns to see the cloud. "Looks like I'm coming with you."

The spacecraft materializes, and they climb in. An army of Grays appears in the distance. Pamuhl fumbles with some switches. "What's this one?"

The army is rapidly approaching as Pamuhl attempts to get the spacecraft going. The first attempt fails. The second and third attempts fail. The army is almost within shooting range. "Concentrate, Pamuhl," demands Zeta.

"Oh, there's an idea," responds Pamuhl. "Well, the only one I haven't tried is this one." She pushes a button.

The Grays begin shooting as the spacecraft starts. Pamuhl counts down, "Three, two, …" She pushes a button, and the spacecraft is gone. The shots fired by the Grays no longer have a target to hit and continue moving across the desert until they contact a cartel vehicle full of cocaine driven by Gray agents. There is an explosion followed by what appears to be a snowstorm.

The Gray army is not certain what has happened. The commanding officer is also confused. The Grays' leadership would not understand failure, so the commanding officer says to the troops, "Good shooting." They all cheer, and the commanding officer reports that the spacecraft has been destroyed.

Pamuhl and Zeta are unaware of the commanding officer's report and believe every Gray spaceship is looking for them. Zeta says, "We must travel away from the beaten path. We'll have to go through unchartered territory."

Pamuhl replies, "That could be riskier than flying through the routes utilized by the Grays."

Zeta tells her, "The odds of us making it to Deltoiga by using conventional routes fall between guaranteed failure and impossible. The only chance we have, though it may be slim, is diving into deep space."

"Better fasten your seat belt," says Pamuhl, turning a knob.

The spacecraft flips upside down. "Oops, wrong knob." Pamhul rights the spacecraft. "Must be this one," she says.

She turns another knob, and the spacecraft hesitates. Pamuhl slaps the controls, and her head snaps back as the craft suddenly jumps to a speed she has never flown at. "The Albie would never go like this," she says. "They really have improved the modern spacecraft."

Pamuhl looks at Zeta and sees concern on his face. "We're not going to make it, are we? Don't worry. Just leave the flying to Pamuhl," she says. "I wonder what this button is for?"

Zeta feels useless. He is helpless and his only hope is to get to a planet he has never been to. There is about to be a crucial battle fought on Earth, and he will not be there for it. The BLR count on him. He feels he is letting them down. Things seem hopeless.

They fly for two days without Gray encounters. "Looks like we're in the clear," states Zeta. "We could probably try and find our way back to a conventional route."

Pamuhl responds, "Yeah, about that. I'm still trying to figure out the navigational system. Nybo had the return coordinates entered in, so we figured it would be a straight shot to Deltoiga. I had to turn the system off to get us into deep space, and when I turned it back on, it was blank. I'll figure it out sooner or later."

Zeta groans and asks, "Can things get any worse?" It will not take long for them to find out.

CHAPTER 20

URSA, NYBO, AND THE DELTOIGANS

Ursa is unsure what she should do, now that she has betrayed the Grays. There are not a lot of useful options for her. Staying at headquarters would drive her crazy; she needs to be moving. Being at any one place for very long gives her cabin fever. Working at a safe house is not her thing, for the same reason. Finding discarded Gray abductees to bring to the safe houses is more to her liking but out of the question. Much too risky. After all, the Grays are looking for her. The other thing that muddies the water is her feelings for Nybo. She has become quite fond of him. It seems he feels the same way about her.

She was able to talk Major Canis into allowing her to escort Nybo and the Deltoigans on their quest to find Jous.

Nybo does not drive, so someone must escort them. She says, "Who can understand Nybo better than me?"

Against objections from almost every BLR bigwig, she is granted her wish. She simply would not take no for an answer. One catch, though: she must wear a disguise. So she now wears a long gray wig and a pair of glasses with lenses as thick as Coke bottles. It gives her the appearance of an old hippie. If she had a ukulele and sang tiptoe through the tulips, she would look like an aged Tiny Tim from the old *Laugh-In* show.

Major Canis has been arguing with BLR leaders that the Grays' retaliation could be more severe than was first expected. The western BLR headquarters could be a target and possibly even the front of a battle. He points out that not all double agents side with the BLR.

The Grays will soon be aware that the BLR, particularly Nybo, and Ursa are to blame for the transport system problems. It is necessary to remove Nybo and Ursa from the danger of the potential upcoming battle. They will travel east and check in at designated BLR bases.

A second driver will go along, someone who could not only be a relief driver, but also serve as a bodyguard for the group. Tiny is selected. Tiny is a two-hundred-sixty-pound Native American who must turn sideways to get through most doors. An intimidating pile of muscle, solid as a rock.

Tiny grew up fighting. During one fight, he popped his opponent's eye out, something he often brags about. One night at a bar, another patron hit him from behind with a beer bottle. Tiny turned and punched the man one time, killing him. Tiny was sentenced to prison for two years but ended up being there for five.

Tiny did not do well in prison. He had a hard time accepting authority. Like most people going to prison for the first time, his plan was to keep to himself and get his time done. With good behavior, he could be out in a year, he thought. Unfortunately, prison does not work that way. The culture sucks a person in. An individual does many things in prison he would never do on the outside. After all, one must survive.

Tiny was quickly sucked in. His celly happened to be a gang member. The gang consisted of all Native Americans. Tiny naturally hung out with the natives, and while he never officially joined the gang, he enjoyed some of the benefits.

One of the gang members who resided on the same unit as Tiny was a small gay man named Ricky. Ricky's celly also happened to be gay, a much bigger and stronger man. He often made unwanted advances toward Ricky. The gang decided the man must be dealt with. While Tiny had no obligations, not being a member, he had received benefits from the gang, things like drugs, porn, and cigarettes. He felt obligated enough that he agreed to deal with the man.

The following day, Ricky left the cell. His celly remained behind, defecating, so his departure was delayed. As Tiny walked by the cell, he saw the man and entered the cell, beating the man senseless while he was still defecating. This incident cost Tiny an additional two years.

In retaliation, three members of a rival gang approached Tiny in the yard attempting to assault him. Tiny sent two of them to the hospital. The third ended up with a traumatic brain injury severe enough that he now resides on a special needs' unit. The man will need care and assistance for the rest of his life. The incident caused Tiny an additional two years.

Tiny was able to stay out of serious trouble after that. He made parole and was released. He returned to the reservation, and his life seemed to pick up where it had left off. Finding work was difficult; not because he had killed another member of the tribe, but because he had killed a member of the

Blackhawk family. The Blackhawk family is well established. Several of them are council members. They run the casino and most of the businesses on the reservation. No way any of them would hire Tiny.

Tiny ended up using a friend from prison to make a connection with a drug dealer. Tiny became the number one guy on the reservation to go to for all your illegal drugs. After all, a man has got to make a living. The tribal judge, the tribal sheriff, and five of the six tribal deputies are also Blackhawks.

Things were going well for Tiny. He had three employees. While the Blackhawks knew he was up to no good, they were unable to catch Tiny doing anything wrong.

One afternoon at a family reunion, Tiny's brother told him he was going to kill one of Tiny's employees. Tiny told his brother that he needed the man and made it clear that he was to be left alone. His brother killed the man anyway. He also killed the man's wife and then went into hiding to avoid retaliation from Tiny.

Tiny left town. He took a long trip, making a large loop through five states. The plan was to make his brother believe he was gone for good. After three weeks, Tiny returned to the reservation. His plan had worked. His brother was no longer in hiding. Tiny entered his brother's house and shot him.

The rule among thugs is that, to avenge a killing, you kill the perpetrator. If the victim's wife was also killed, you avenge that killing as well. Even Steven, which coincidentally was Tiny's brother's name. After shooting his brother, Tiny turned toward his sister-in-law. She stated, "I suppose you're going to kill me now."

Tiny hesitated and said, "No, you have to raise the kids."

Someone once asked Tiny if he killed his brother, and Tiny responded, "I thought I did, but he's just paraplegic and blind. And don't you know, the bitch left him after three months."

The killing was all the Blackhawks needed. Tiny got word they were coming for him, so he fled the reservation. While driving through the desert one night, a strange object appeared in the sky. A bright light encompassed his vehicle and he was off to Betelgeuse for three years that he cannot remember. He was dropped in Mexico and found by Zeta before the Grays on Earth could get to him.

The group enters the van. Tiny takes the entire back seat so he can halfway lie down. The nuns all pile in the remaining two rows of bench seats. Ursa and Nybo sit in bucket seats in the front. They begin their quest east to find Jous by taking a similar route to Moe, Joe, and Cindy.

The van is abuzz as the five nuns talk away and ask questions. None of them have ever left Deltoiga before. They all have a mixed feeling of confusion and awe. They are overwhelmed by Earth.

Some of them are not completely convinced they can trust Nybo. They were brought here, after all, by their new friends, the Grays. As the ride continues, they get more and more excited about Earth.

Nybo explains some of the customs Earthlings have. He tells them, "Wait till you try the coffee." He then tells them about his trek across the desert and how he was picked up.

He asks the nuns if a man named John Smith had ever come to Deltoiga for vacation. As Nybo continues speaking about his adventures, he suddenly becomes homesick. Sitting back in his seat, his expression changes from happy to concerned. "What's wrong?" asks Ursa.

Nybo responds, "I really miss home. I was so close to returning. Now, I have no idea if I'll ever get back there. It depends on Pamuhl and Fraxel being successful, not only on their journey, but in convincing Albie III and the Wisdom Core that the Grays aren't who they say they are. We aren't even certain they'll make it. If they don't, there won't be a shuttle sent to pick us up." Ursa slides her hand into Nybo's, and they lock fingers.

They stop at the same dinner Moe, Joe, and Cindy had. The nuns try coffee for the first time. They do not want to leave, and they continue drinking coffee until Tiny insists they must go.

Barely back on the road, Sister Anna says, "I need to use a restroom." The other nuns agree. They stop at the gas station where Joe met Star. The clerk at the gas station cannot keep the coffee pot full. He makes pot after pot as fast as he can. He looks at Tiny and asks, "What is it with nuns and coffee?"

Tiny shrugs his shoulders. "How should I know? I'm not Catholic." Once again, he insists they get going.

On the road for less than a half hour, Sister Agnes states, "I have to use a restroom." Of course, the other nuns agree. Tiny agrees to stop at a gas station but tells them no more coffee for today. They are all disappointed but realize Tiny will not stop unless they agree. As the nuns come out of the ladies' room, Tiny uses the mens' room.

Four motorcycles pull into the station. The riders are members of the Gray Devils, a gang with a bad reputation, no relation to the Grays. Seeing five nuns, they decide to have some fun. One of the gang pats Sister Abigail on her backside. While laughing, he says, "I never had me a penguin before. You ready to find out what a man can do?" The other gang members laugh.

Nybo steps in and says, "You have no idea who you're messing with."

As Tiny exits the restroom, he sees two of the gang members pick Nybo up and throw him into a dumpster. Another one of the gang members begins harassing Ursa. She produces a container of chemical spray and shoots the man directly in the eyes, causing one of the others to slap her.

Tiny emerges from inside of the station. He walks over to the dumpster and lifts Nybo out using only one hand. He turns to Ursa and sees her cheek is beginning to swell and her glasses are broken. One of the gang members tells him, "Stay out of this if you know what's good for yoooafff."

Tiny punches him before he can finish his sentence, knocking him five feet backward. The man lands on all fours and cannot breathe or get up. Another gang member pulls out a knife. Tiny lifts one of their bikes and throws it at him. The gang member's jaw drops in awe, and the knife falls to the ground. Tiny then throws a bike into the dumpster, followed by the man who had gotten sprayed in the eyes.

The Deltoigans enter the van along with Ursa and Tiny. They resume their journey, with Nybo and Ursa hugging and consoling each other. The gang members are left in awe, now with two damaged bikes and two damaged members. They manage to get a good look at the van and the license plate.

The word gets out quickly. The Gray Devils form search groups of ten to twelve members, and the hunt is on. Rule number two is no one messes with a Gray Devil. Rule number one is no one messes with a Gray Devil's bike.

The van continues down the highway. The nuns are getting edgy and cranky, coming down from a caffeine buzz. Ursa's cheek is swollen, and she is beginning to get a black eye. "We'll have to stop and get ice," states Tiny.

A pack of Gray Devils heading west zoom by the van. After a short distance, they stop and one of them pulls out a piece of paper with the license plate number. "I think that might be them," he tells the others. They turn around and pursue the van.

Tiny slows down, as there are several large cattle walking onto the road. They are part of a herd being driven by four cowboys on horseback. The van drives by them before the entire herd walks onto the road. The herd follows the road, and the Gray Devils pull up behind them. One of the cowboy's waves to the Gray Devils to drive into and through the herd.

Driving through the herd, the Gray Devils get separated. The cattle are taller than their bikes, and the Gray Devils are unable to see anything. The van exits onto another highway, which has a gas station a mile away. The Gray Devils do not notice as they continue to struggle their way through the cattle. Clearing the herd, they are well beyond the road where the van turned. They speed down the highway, pursuing a vehicle which is no longer ahead of them.

The van pulls into the gas station with the occupants unaware they are being pursued by Gray Devils. Ursa gets ice to help reduce the effects of the slap.

The nuns beg Tiny to allow them to have more coffee. Tiny has a headache from them being so cranky and decides it is the only way he will get any peace. Tiny tells them, "Since we'll need to stop for a restroom break, I'm taking us to Tashunka Witko. No other breaks until we get there.

Nybo asks, "What's Twoshoie with o?"

Tiny corrects him, "Not what, who. Tashunka Witko, Crazy Horse, the great chief of the Oglala. He's being immortalized on a mountain. It's near a small BLR base where we can spend the night."

The van arrives at the monument, and the nuns rush into the restroom. Tiny, Ursa, and Nybo begin talking about their journey. Ursa mentions that it is both nice and weird they haven't encountered any Grays. Tiny reminds her that the others have gone ahead of them taking a similar route. "We don't know if anything has happened between them and the Grays," he says. This causes Nybo to worry about his friends.

The nuns return, and the group looks at the monument. Tiny tells them the story of Little Big Horn. The Deltoigans are impressed that mountains look like people. There are no mountains on Deltoiga. The highest point of elevation is twenty-two feet. It is a sacred spot. Deltoigans come from all over the planet to see it.

As night begins to fall, the group leaves the monument and heads down the road. After a short drive, they arrive at the back side of Mount Rushmore where they enter a well-hidden cave and are met by BLR members. Following formalities, they are treated to dinner, spaghetti.

The group dines with General Gemini. During the meal, he updates them on the several skirmishes with the Grays that have already taken place. He tells them no updates have been received about Zeta, Pamuhl or Fraxel. "Once the others are on their way, Zeta will report to a safe house located near the spacecraft," he tells them. "We should be receiving word on him within a day or two."

General Gemini congratulates Nybo and Ursa on the success of their mission, which has disrupted the Grays' transportation system. "We won a great battle which was intended to delay their plan to take over Earth. Unfortunately, their reaction was greater than expected. I'm afraid it turns out we have thrown a spark into a powder keg."

General Gemini informs them of the massive incoming fleet of Gray spacecraft over the last couple of evenings. "They were planning on taking over Earth, now they're planning a war with the BLR, which could very well destroy Earth. The risk of your journey has increased greatly. There was talk of cancelling it. However, for now, you are to continue. You must be extremely cautious. Do nothing to attract attention to yourselves."

The following morning, the group prepares for their departure. Nybo, Ursa, and Tiny are issued weapons by a BLR field instructor, the new Spontaneous Combustor SC2 ray gun. Following a brief practice session, they are ready to depart. Tiny states, "I hope those nuns are quiet today. I'm tired of questions and hearing about Deltoiga."

The nuns had several cups of coffee at breakfast. They are waiting in the van singing one thousand bottles of beer on the wall. Each with a thirty-two-ounce to-go cup filled with coffee.

CHAPTER 21

PLANNING FOR TROUBLE

It is a calm, clear night on Deltoiga. The *Daily Deltoigan* newspaper features photos of several of the Wisdom Core members posing with Will Robinson and other Gray ambassadors. There is an article speaking of the sudden departure of the Grays and the threat posed to Deltoiga and other planets by Earthlings. Deltoiga's new friends, the Grays, will be dealing with the evil Earthlings and, afterward, will return to Deltoiga to once again enlighten the population with the technology they share, improving the lives of Deltoigan citizens.

There is another article speaking of the Deltoigan ambassadors who are brave enough, and lucky enough, to be participating on a voyage to tour a planet inhabited by the Grays. They will witness firsthand the utopia the Grays have created and are willing to share, not only with Deltoiga but also with people and planets everywhere. The article continues by asking readers to check future editions for updates—the Wisdom Core is expecting a report from the ambassadors soon.

The Wisdom Core is about to hold a meeting. The agenda includes discussion about Nybo, the renegade voyager, Pamuhl, and what can be done to show appreciation to the Grays for their friendship.

The Wisdom Supreme calls the meeting to order, but before he can bring up the first item on the agenda, he is interrupted with a question from one of the members, "What's that you're wearing around your neck?" Deltoigans have never heard of jewelry.

The Wisdom Supreme answers, "Oh, this was a gift from one of the Gray ambassadors. They call it bling. They traded it for a useless patch of land on the north side of the planet."

The other members ooh and ahh as they see it. "Did they give you anymore?" asks another member.

The Wisdom Supreme responds, "No, just this one."

Soon every member of the Core states, "I want bling."

The Wisdom Supreme responds, "When they return, we'll ask them for more."

A member replies, "Why don't we share that one?"

The Wisdom supreme answers, "Well, they gave it to me. I'm sure they intended for it to be mine." Jealousy, envy, and greed are traits not often found on Deltoiga, but the entire meeting is filled with them.

The meeting goes on for hours, with members proposing ways the bling could be shared. The Wisdom Supreme is unwilling to listen. A deep divide is driven between everyone in attendance. Every member feels they should be the first to wear the bling, while the Wisdom Supreme argues against it. The meeting adjourns without a single agenda item being discussed.

The members exit the Wisdom cave, and the pleas to share the bling continue. The Wisdom Supreme asks everyone to keep their thoughts down as he points out, "We don't want everyone to know about unfinished business." The Wisdom Supreme swiftly walks away.

One of the members suggests to the others, "Maybe we'll just have to take it from him." During the entire existence of Deltoiga, there has never been a stolen item; Deltoigans do not even know what stealing is.

Meanwhile on Betelgeuse, a meeting of the military leaders is held to discuss the best course of action for dealing with Earth. King Alpha, head of the royal family, is attending. He is very upset with the latest developments and wants vengeance immediately.

King Alpha usually leaves military operations to his generals. When things go smoothly, the king is content; but when there's failure, he becomes irrational and angry, which does not end well for those involved. Failure normally results in execution.

The king's fist come down heavily on the table. "Who's responsible for this? I was told the leadership of Earth was ours and the takeover was ready to begin! Now you're telling me someone allowed our transport system to be breached! Who's responsible?" The generals sink down in their seats, afraid to speak. The king begins to turn colors with anger.

One of the generals gets enough nerve to respond, "Sire, the general in charge of the far south sector isn't here today."

"Very well, you'll do. Freeze and burn him," responds the king while pointing at the general brave enough to speak.

Freeze and burn is a torturous, painful, humiliating death. The victim is frozen and placed in public, where a passerby can spit or urinate on him, causing slight melting and making the victim feel like he is being burned by acid. At the end of the day, a crowd gathers to watch the executioner light a torch and slowly melt the individual. First melting fingers, then toes, then the nose and face. The crowd cheers while the victim melts in extreme pain. The execution ends with the genitals being melted and the remains thrown into a large bonfire.

The king looks at the remaining generals and asks what is being done about Earth. The general in charge of environments and land sciences states, "Sire, Dr. Wind's global warming plan is coming along nicely. There are leaders on Earth who estimate an end to life in ten to twelve years. If we step the program up, it could be cut to eight years without too much damage to the planet's resources."

Shaking his head, the king says, "No, no. That's too long. We need to deliver a message, not only to Earth, but to planets everywhere. Nobody messes with the king! I mean, the Grays."

One of the generals states, "Sire, through years of experimentation, we've learned a great deal about the genetic makeup of Earthlings. We have been preparing a biological contamination program which would substantially reduce the population. We have also developed a gene-altering additive which could be introduced into the Earthlings food chain, weakening future generations." He continues. "Our cartel operations are shipping drugs around Earth at a record pace. The drugs continue to increase in strength and are causing a record number of overdoses."

The king is growing frustrated. "Long-range plans should continue, but we have to act now." The king states, "Let's just blow Earth up and move on!"

A general reminds the king of the valuable resources Earth can provide. Another suggests the planet could be useful as a substation, providing opportunity for expansion of the Grays' realm.

The general states, "I recommend we send an army to Earth. The BLR has been expanding their operations there. The first wave sent can begin hunting them down. It will appear as a small-scale reaction to their attack on our transport system, allowing us time to put together an intergalactic alliance. We can then begin a full-scale invasion, surprising the BLR and eliminating them." The other generals nod their heads in agreement.

The king states, "Go on."

The general continues. "We'll send a couple of battalions from Betelgeuse and Rigel, big enough to make the BLR believe it's our reaction to their attack on our transport system. While we put together an alliance, a supply chain can be developed going through Alpha Centauri, the most central location for this battle. Within two weeks, we can launch a full-scale attack, eliminating the BLR. By the time the Earthlings can react, the BLR on Earth will be eliminated. We then enslave the local population and help ourselves to their resources."

The king laughs and claps his hands. "Very good. You have one week."

The general reacts by stating, "Sire, I was hoping to use General Bootes from the Vega operation in the north sector. It will take a little time for his replacement to get there and make him available."

The king hastily reacts, "Vega is becoming a thorn. The juice isn't worth the squeeze. Have General Bootes blow it up and report here immediately."

"As you wish, sire," responds the general. Vega is blown up the next day. The act will later bring unforeseen consequences.

The BLR are having a meeting of their own. They recognize that war with the Grays is imminent, so they have been preparing as best they can. The question is where and when? As the Grays begin putting their plan into action, BLR surveillance suggests that something is likely to happen soon. All indicators point to Earth.

The BLR armies are spread throughout the multiverse, small bans of rebels nagging and disrupting the Grays operations. The BLR recognizes that they are underequipped and outnumbered. Observing the movement of the Grays' allies, it appears that Earth will soon be overrun with enemy forces. Whatever troops the BLR send there are sure to be defeated along with the troops already there.

General Lyra states, "Our best chance for saving Earth and ourselves is to do what we have always done, disrupt and distract. With all the manpower and firepower the Grays are sending to Earth, we don't stand a chance by engaging in a full-scale battle."

The top two strategist for the BLR, General Caster and General Auriga, speak up.

General Caster presents, "We send enough of our armies to Earth to make the Grays believe we're going to try and fight them. While we'll be fighting there, we hold back enough of our armies to fight their allies on their own planets. You see, we let the allied planets send the first couple of waves of armies without interference. Once they're well on their way, we attack the planets and their remaining armies. Their armies will be at half strength, giving us the advantage. The results are twofold. The armies headed to Earth will return to defend their own planet, which denies the Grays expected reinforcements, and we'll have caused extensive damage to the planet and armies who remained. We'll be gone before the returning armies arrive."

General Lyra is concerned about sending troops to Earth; but he likes the idea of fighting half armies. He turns to General Auriga and asks, "What have you got for us?"

General Auriga responds, "I believe we can distract Betelgeuse and Rigel, forcing them to send troops elsewhere. Give me twenty-four hours to get the logistics together, and I'll confirm my plan."

"Very well," states General Lyra. "Gentlemen, the fate of every planet everywhere lies in our hands. We must not—cannot—fail. Prepare your troops. Tomorrow, we go to war."

Nybo, Ursa, Tiny, and the nuns are eating cheeseburgers. A nearby band of Gray Devils are eating spaghetti. If they had ridden two more miles before stopping, they would have found the van.

The nuns start dreaming up different foods. "How about spaghetti burgers," suggests Sister Ariel.

Sister Anna adds, "Yes, with the noodles boiled in coffee."

Tiny can barely swallow.

CHAPTER 22

THE QUIET BEFORE THE STORM

Scientists and meteorologists are presenting various theories about the continuing meteorite showers being observed on Earth each dusk till dawn. Prognosticators, as they have done since the beginning, tell us it is the end of times, the end of Earth.

It is all hype. Doomsday predictions will always be wrong. If they ever happen to be right, nobody will know, everyone would be dead.

The van full of Deltoigans and friends continues eastward. Nybo moves his arm and bumps his elbow against the weapon he now possesses, the first weapon he has ever had.

The radio is on, and the news talks about North Korean missile tests, unrest between Hong Kong and China, the ongoing threat of Russia and Putin, murders in Mexico, and the number of shooting deaths that occurred over the weekend in Chicago and Baltimore.

Nybo states, "You know, Deltoiga is peaceful all the time, not like Earth. The people on Earth don't realize that peace is there; it's a given. It's the people of Earth who disturb the peace, they won't allow it. Maybe they need to observe an international day of peace, a day where everybody from all nations stay at home and be calm. The people of Earth could get a little taste of the peace that's always there. You just have to allow it." Tiny mumbles something in his native language, which nobody understands.

Tiny states, "You don't understand the natural order of living things. Take eagles, for example. If there are three eaglets in the nest and the mother is finding plenty of food, they're happy and content. If the mother is struggling to find food and the eaglets are hungry, they push each other out of the nest. Same with humans. When they have everything they need, they share and get along. When there are shortages, they become savages and fight for things."

Sister Abigale says, "I don't understand why they would do that. On Deltoiga, we share everything."

Tiny responds, "It's called survival. So long as there's survival, there won't be peace."

Tiny says, "I'm just saying that peace isn't as easy as you think. It's unnatural to living things. My fathers and their fathers before them shared everything. Any animal killed was shared among the tribe. An animal pelt was given to the one who needed it most, for garments or moccasins. They grew gardens, and everyone reaped the benefits."

Tiny continues. "Peaceful, right? But the world is bigger than your own living room. There were other tribes whose fathers and their fathers before them roamed the countryside. They were nomads who were out for themselves. They would raid the gardens of my fathers, taking what they could carry and destroying the rest, leaving my tribe to starve. That is how they survived. That is just the way things are."

Nybo replies, "Oh."

On Betelgeuse, the eight-year-old girls An and Na are playing with dolls. One doll has a human male body with a frog head; the other has a horse body with the head of a human woman. They pretend the two dolls are going on a date. The two girls play all day, oblivious to the military affairs taking place.

On Deltoiga, the two eight-year-old twins Mar and Tha are baking *soilo* pies in their easy-bake nuclear oven. Soilo pies are comparable to mud pies. The girls will soon talk six-year-old Stash, the boy who lives next door, into trying one. They are oblivious to Earth and Betelgeuse.

On Earth the two eight-year-old girls Jewel and Lee are playing a card game called war. Their mother keeps telling them to play nice and stop arguing. The game ends when Jewel punches Lee on the arm and she runs away crying. The two girls are oblivious to Betelgeuse and Deltoiga and anything else without a price tag.

Moe, Joe, Cindy and Star, still being tracked by a Gray drone, are almost to Minneapolis. They need to make a rest stop and end up at the Spam museum. They enter the museum at the same time the tracking drone is running out of battery power. The drone heads for a Gray base while a replacement drone heads for the museum.

A car thief enters the Camaro and drives out of the parking lot just as the replacement drone arrives. The drone begins tracking the Camaro. After thirty-five minutes the Camaro arrives at a garage and beeps the horn. An overhead door opens, and the Camaro enters the building. The overhead door closes, and the drone continues to hover over the garage.

Moe, Joe, Cindy, and Star exit the museum to find an empty parking space. "Oh great!" exclaims Moe. "My Camaro." He fights breaking into tears.

Star asks, "Are you going to call the police?"

"And tell them what?" Moe asks. "That we are on our way to a safe house to cleanse the minds of victims of alien abductions. Probably not recommended. Besides one of us might be a person of interest to the police. Something about an unfulfilled commitment."

Joe contacts the BLR, and after receiving a brief chewing out, he is instructed to sit tight. The four of them are in luck. The BLR has a small base located below the Spam museum. A car arrives in minutes, and the four travelers are on their way with strict instructions not to make any stops.

Will Robinson is on Earth and learns of the pink Camaro and how oddly the occupants acted during the encounters with the Gray agents from the restaurant. He orders the Camaro destroyed and adds, "Make it look like an accident, and be sure all of them are in the car." His logic is that even if the four riders are not working for the BLR, Earthlings will soon be eliminated anyway. Might as well start early.

A small force of Gray soldiers storm the garage containing the Camaro and begin to shoot anything that moves, killing everyone. One of the Grays is killed and another injured. The Gray force exits the garage as a midsize battle craft arrives and fires a greenish ray at the garage, causing it to vanish. There are several UFO sightings reported to authorities and the media by local witnesses.

The Grays are attacking suspected BLR hideouts. Will Robinson oversees the operation. He is being very aggressive and is unconcerned that the attacks are often against innocent humans.

The leaders on Earth are asking the Gray leaders what is happening. They are reassured by the Grays that a routine military drill is taking place. It is for the protection and well-being of Earth. The Grays give each of the leaders millions of dollars and reinforce the notion that they will soon be given power to rule over the universe.

A small band of Gray Devils spot the van with the nuns. The van approaches a railroad crossing, and as they drive over the tracks, red lights begin to flash and loud bells ring. The train arrives at the crossing simultaneously with the Gray Devils. The Gray Devils are forced to wait for the train to pass. They are oblivious to Betelgeuse and Deltoiga and the battle about to take place.

The traffic in outer space is heavy as spacecraft from the Grays' alliance begin their journey to Earth. The supply line to Earth from Alpha Centauri has begun operating. King Alpha is in the vault playing with his treasure. He is oblivious to how things are going.

In deep space, Pamuhl and Zeta remain lost. While they are aware of an impending battle about to take place on Earth, they are more concerned about their own survival. They are oblivious to how their situation is about to change.

CHAPTER 23

DEEP SPACE

Pamuhl is worried, yet confident she can figure out the navigational system. Their fate is in her hands. They are both developing cabin fever, and Zeta is getting edgy. Being lost gives them a sinking feeling. Zeta suggest they go in a different direction, which they do until Pamuhl says, I really think we are better off going this way, which they do. Soon the spacecraft is going in circles, getting nowhere.

Pamuhl excitedly exclaims, "I think I've got it," believing she has figured out the navigational system.

Zeta points. "Set it to go this way."

Pamuhl recognizes there is something different about the way he pointed. A slight blurry streak followed his hand movement, and when it stopped, his whole hand was a blur.

He turns his head to look at Pamuhl, and the movement is followed by a blurry streak. Now his entire body is a blur.

He looks at Pamuhl. "Pamuhl what are you doing? You are all blurry."

Pamuhl looks down at her hand and sees a blur. She moves it, observing a blurry streak. She breathlessly asks, "What's going on?"

Looking at the control panel, they see a blurry mess of knobs, buttons, and levers. When reaching for something, their vision perceives there should be contact, but the hand seems to reach all the way through the object before there is contact.

The two voyagers are in a panic as perception and reality have separated. Concentrating on remaining calm is exhausting but necessary to avoid a panicked outburst. As fear builds to a crescendo, the mind feels as though it could leave the body and things would be normal. These crescendos keep reoccurring every few seconds. Communicating with each other results in panic, so they find it best to remain quiet and focused on trying to stay calm.

Continuing their journey to who knows where, they begin to perceive that the spacecraft is standing still and all the planets and stars are moving. Their minds are at a breaking point when Pamuhl says, "I can't take this anymore. We've got to stop."

Zeta responds, "I know how you feel. That looks like a planet over there. Let's go for it."

Pamuhl looks through the blurry streaks that follow every star and sees a small blue ball in the distance. Grabbing the blurry steering stick, she guides the craft toward the planet. She anticipates relief from the unfamiliar perceptions her mind has been wrestling with. As the blue ball grows larger, she thinks back to being stranded on Earth's moon. She wonders if the planet will have any life.

Pamuhl fumbles around the dashboard and gropes for a knob before pulling on a lever that causes the craft to slow down. Entering the gravitational pull of the planet, the spacecraft shakes and jerks. There is no way to be sure where the blur ends and the planet begins, so the landing is rough but successful.

Looking out from the spacecraft, the planet is a blur. The craft being static rather than dynamic helps a little, but their depth perception continues to tax their minds. Observing blurry boulders and blurry hills full of blurry, lush, brown trees, Pamuhl asks, "Should we step outside?"

Zeta responds, "What have we got to lose?"

On Earth, the nuns are down to two hundred eighty-nine bottles of beer on the wall. Ursa and Nybo are riding in the back seat of the van. Ursa places her arm around Nybo, who looks into her lemon-yellow eyes. The two tightly embrace before locking lips in a world record long kiss. Tiny cannot take the music anymore and stops for a break at a scenic overlook.

Seconds later, the spaghetti-eating band of Gray Devils stop at the scenic overlook. Seeing the van, they cannot believe their luck. "Let's bust up some nuns," says one of them.

The leader of the band, who prides himself in fighting, says, "The Indian is mine."

Tiny has walked away from the group, trying to regain his patience. The Gray Devils surround Nybo, Ursa, and the nuns. "Say your prayers," states one of the gang members. "And I don't mean the rosary."

Nybo does not think about the weapon he possesses but recalls how scared Joe had gotten at the hospital when he saw a natural Deltoigan form. He instructs the nuns to change to their natural Deltoigan forms. The gang members are dumbstruck and step back. "What the h-e-hockey-sticks is this?"

Tiny appears and grabs the leader from behind, throwing him like a sack of potatoes. The other gang members run to their bikes. The leader gets up, too confused to fight, and runs to his bike. The Gray Devils leave the scenic stop and race away as fast as their bikes will go. The Deltoigans convert back to their nun forms and climb into the van, resuming their song.

The Gray Devils get about ten miles before being pulled over by the police. The officer does not feel like dealing with a bunch of disrespectful gang members, so he decides he will simply give them a warning and ask them to slow down. He cautiously approaches the gang who all begin talking at him at once. They are ranting, telling him about the nuns and how they switched to aliens.

The officer asks the Gray Devils to stay where they are as he returns to the patrol car and calls for backup. He tells dispatch, "I don't know what these guys are on, but it must be something good." Backup arrives and the gang is searched for drugs. Nine of eleven members are arrested.

Zeta and Pamuhl cannot accurately perceive where the ground begins and the blur ends, causing them to stumble out of the spacecraft. The yellow grass is coarse and crunches under their feet. They find the atmosphere is user-friendly.

Each time they turn their heads, there is a blurry streak that follows their eyes. When their heads stop, there is just blurry. They take small steps to get their feet acquainted with the ground. It is determined that if they do not look down, walking is easier.

Stopping at a twenty-foot-tall tree, they see fruit resembling bananas. Pamuhl reaches for one but misses on the first try. She is successful on her next attempt and plucks one from the tree. Peeling back the skin she states, "It smells like a banana. If it looks like a banana, feels like a banana, and smells like a banana, then it's probably a banana. I'll give it a taste."

Zeta cautions her, "Bananas aren't blurry. Take a very small taste and wait awhile. See how it affects your system."

Walking over a couple of brushy hills, they locate a blurry lake, where they take a break. Zeta sticks his hand into the orange-colored water. Lifting his hand out of the lake, he smells the orange droplets on his fingers. "Smells fresh," he states before licking some of the droplets. "Tastes like the water on Earth," he concludes.

Getting out of the spacecraft has given them a refreshed feeling and an improved attitude. Zeta asks, "Pamuhl, do you really think you'll be able to get the navigational system going?"

Pamuhl answers, "Ninety-nine percent guaranteed, although the best I can do is plug in the location of Deltoiga. I don't have a starting point, and who knows how the ship will respond in this blurry place? Don't worry. Like I said, seventy-nine percent guaranteed."

Neither of them is ready to climb back into the spacecraft. Without discussion, they gather firewood and start a fire. Pamuhl seems to be full of energy after tasting the blurry banana, and she has not experienced any side effects. Finding roasting sticks, they impale the blurry bananas and roast them over the fire.

While they sit spellbound by the blurry fire, Pamuhl asks, "What's your story, Zeta? How did you come to be a member of the BLR?"

Zeta stares at the fire. "Once there were more than a few cultures existing within the Orion region of space. They lived in peace and harmony, resembling the way you describe Deltoiga. One planet and its culture were technologically advanced to the others. In the beginning, they shared their technology with the entire region. Then greed set in, and they started trading for it. Once they realized their culture was the most powerful in the region, they kept the technology to themselves and began taking."

"What planet was that?" asks Pamuhl.

"Betelgeuse," replies Zeta.

"The Grays?" she asks.

"Yes," he answers.

After a pause Pamuhl asks, "And then?"

Zeta responds, "The other planets pleaded with Betelgeuse to stop harvesting their resources. Had they only known what was to come, they may have been able to form an alliance and stop the Grays."

"Why didn't they?" she asks.

Zeta continues. "The planets in the region had a trusting nature that the Grays used against them. You are aware that the Grays lack emotion and empathy. They had no problem telling the planets of the region what they wanted to hear. Making promises they had no intention of keeping.

"Those bass turds," says Pamuhl, believing she is swearing.

Zeta looks at her. "I believe I know what you're trying to say."

Returning his attention to the fire, he continues. "By the time the other planets figured out things weren't going to change, it was too late. The Grays enslaved them and used them to do the labor. They were forced to rape their own planets of its resources, gaining nothing and living under martial law."

Following another pause, Pamuhl says, "That still doesn't answer my question."

Zeta replies, "No, I guess not." He continues. "My great-great- grandfather, Abuelo, was a leader on the planet Granite. He was away trying to warn other planets of the Grays and form an alliance against them. The Grays came looking for him. After mercilessly torturing other leaders on Granite, the Grays learned of my great-great-grandfather's mission." Tears develop in Zeta's eyes, and his voice becomes shaky as he says, "They blew up Granite." He chokes while saying, "They blew up the whole planet. Eliminated a whole race."

The planet grows dark for the evening. Plans can be made in the morning as both Pamuhl and Zeta are mentally exhausted. Having full stomachs, they feel content and fall into a deep sleep under the stars. They are oblivious to the fact they are being watched.

A maximum-power Betelgeusian battle craft, capable of blowing up an entire planet, is en route to Earth. Will Robinson continues to hunt the BLR, destroying small bases and killing most people. A few BLR members are spared for questioning. The questioning sessions start out nice but end with the subject being submitted to extreme torture. They eventually give the location of other BLR bases.

Melvin works for the BLR driving a delivery vehicle resembling a UPS van. He stops at several of the BLR bases and safe houses. Melvin had the misfortune of being at a location that was attacked by the Grays. He was taken prisoner and delivered to Will Robinson for questioning.

The interrogation begins nicely. Will Robinson offers Melvin cake and coffee. Will Robinson attempts to woo

Melvin and persuade him the Grays are good and the BLR is evil. Melvin is not persuaded and offers tidbits of misinformation. Ten minutes later, an executioner arrives and the real interrogation begins.

Melvin finds himself hanging over a large vat of boiling oil as Will Robinson asks questions. When an answer is unacceptable, the executioner lowers Melvin closer to the vat. If Melvin does not give an answer, the executioner lowers him.

Melvin's feet are inches above the boiling oil. He can no longer handle the pain as the bottoms of his feet are scorching from the rising heat, and he begins talking. Will Robinson thanks Melvin for the information and then nods his head toward the executioner, who lowers Melvin until his feet are within an inch of the oil. "You know more," states Will Robinson.

Melvin insists he has told all he knows. The executioner lowers Melvin so the bottoms of his feet are in the boiling oil. Melvin screams from the excruciating pain. After several seconds, Melvin is lifted. The bottoms of his feet are melted as they hang inches above the vat in the rising heat. Fighting to retain consciousness, Melvin gives Will Robinson the location of several safe houses, including the one in Minneapolis. Will Robinson says, "You know more."

Melvin cries out, "No, no, that's everything!"

He is lowered into the boiling oil until only the tops of his feet are exposed. After several seconds, he is lifted. He dangles three feet above the vat, getting a break from the raising heat.

Will Robinson says, "How rude of me. You must be hot. Here is a fan to help cool you off."

A strong burst of wind hits Melvin's melted feet causing him to lose consciousness. The executioner is able to revive Melvin, and Will Robinson states, "This isn't necessary. Tell me what you know, and we can take care of your foot problem.

I like you, Melvin. I'd hate to see you go through more pain." Melvin insists he has told all he knows.

The executioner slowly lowers Melvin toward the oil. Melvin screams and begs to be spared. Will Robinson gives him another chance to share more information. Melvin tells him he has told all he knows and is dipped midway up his shins. Giving a final scream, Melvin passes out from the agony. Lifted out once again, Melvin hangs above the oil. The executioner is unable to revive him. Will Robinson nods, and Melvin is completely submerged into the vat.

The UFO reports are piling up on Earth. Each day more calls are received than the previous day. The world leaders are asking questions but are easily convinced that everything taking place is for their own protection and wellbeing. The world leaders are even assisting the Grays by providing old airfields and shutdown military bases.

The BLR on Earth are franticly requesting reinforcements and supplies. They have been attacking a few of the smaller Gray bases but are having little impact due to the number of Gray soldiers arriving daily. Over half of the smaller BLR bases have been attacked. A few of the better equipped bases were able to fight and force the Grays to retreat. Most were not so lucky, with all soldiers who were present being killed and the base destroyed.

Will Robinson recognizes that it is time to strike larger BLR bases. He places the Gray armies on hold for a couple of days allowing time for supplies and allies to arrive.

The supply line from Alpha Centauri is humming. The Allies are well on their way and should be arriving in the next day or two. General Bootes has just landed.

Morning arrives on planet blurry. Pamuhl and Zeta arise to a beautiful but blurry sunny day. "What shall we have for breakfast?" asks Pamuhl.

"Blurry bananas," answers Zeta.

They sit next to the lake, eating blurry bananas and deciding on a plan. The only certainty is that they will take some blurry bananas with them.

Neither of them is prepared to enter the spacecraft, but they must get to Deltoiga. Looking out on the lake for the last time, Pamuhl states, "You know, this is the most relaxed I've felt since I left Deltoiga."

They walk over hills and stop to pick a dozen bananas. Walking toward the spacecraft, they stop as someone is approaching them. The man is four and a half feet tall and dressed in a white robe. He is holding a staff. His face has humanlike features; however, his nose sticks out about four inches. Under a head of messy green hair, his blue eyes look them over.

He introduces himself as Pabloba. Zeta and Pamuhl introduce themselves and begin asking questions. Looking away from Pabloba they see that twenty other four-and-a-half-foot, green-haired, blue-eyed, big-nosed people dressed in white robes have joined them.

Pabloba explains that they are on the planet Yinyang. He invites them for a beverage referred to as *aet*. Walking a short distance over a couple of heavily wooded hills, they enter a cave. Following a narrow passage for a short distance, they arrive at a large, round, well-lit area full of hustling Yinyangites all dressed in white robes with similar features to Pabloba and the others. The Yinyangites are followed by a blurry trail as they move swiftly through the room.

The room is filled with occupied tables and humming with conversation. There's art on the wall, depicting stick people on a journey. One picture has a single stick person on top of a mountain addressing a crowd of stick people down below. Another depicts stick people crossing a river while holding large sacks and baskets over their heads. Another has stick people on their knees. They appear to be praying. There are at least twenty pictures.

Pamuhl, Zeta, and Pabloba are joined by two other Yinyangites as they sit at one of the tables. They are served immediately. While they drink aet and eat a yinyangian favorite called *setad*, Pabloba says, "You are from the third dimension. We have heard of your kind but have never met one of you."

While reaching for and missing her aet cup, Pamuhl asks, "Why is everything so blurry?"

One of the other Yinyangites answers, "To you, things appear blurry, to us, things are perfectly normal. You're the ones who are out of focus."

Zeta states, "So we're in the fourth dimension."

Pabloba responds, "Don't be silly. You wouldn't last a minute in the fourth dimension. This is more like the third and a half dimension, a transitional buffer zone."

Pabloba tells them, "You don't know how lucky you are to have landed on this side of the planet. Here we have moral codes. The great prophet Sesom was given ten commandments from the creator of all things, Dog. On this side of the planet, we honor them. The other side of the planet is pure evil. It's in a constant state of chaos, inhabited by lawless heathens. It's ruled by Natas, the devil himself. Had you landed there, you would have been beaten, robbed, and most likely be dead now."

Zeta asks, "How is it that you heard of third-dimensional people?"

Pabloba answers, "You have been talked about several times at the United Planets meetings. One of the member planets, Mir, is close to the border with the third dimension. The third-dimension planet, Vega, is close to the border, and the two planets have become allies. Mir brings lots of news of the third dimension."

Pamuhl sees the opportunity to get back to the third dimension and possibly find their way to Deltoiga. "Can you tell us how to get to Mir?" she asks.

"Of course," states Pabloba. "But pleasure before business. Come now, we'll take a tour. Later, there will be a church service followed by a feast in your honor. We'll discuss business tomorrow."

As the tour on Yinyang begins, Moe, Joe, Cindy, and Star arrive at the safe house. After a cold reception, they are shown to their rooms. They are given a quick tour and shown to their work area. Told they will begin work in one hour, they are introduced to the house director, Kappa.

Kappa looks at Star, believing she was brought to the safe house to be cleansed and asks," What planet are you from?"

Star gives her usual response, "Men are from Mars; women are from Venus."

Kappa asks, "How long were you there for?" Star looks confused. Kappa turns to Moe and asks, "Where did you find her?"

Moe tells him, "She was stranded at a gas station in South Dakota, so we brought her here."

"Odd place for the Grays to drop someone, but good work," says Kappa.

CHAPTER 24

THE WAR BEGINS

General Bootes immediately establishes he is in charge. He calls Will Robinson to a private meeting, and within minutes, it is obvious the two personalities conflict. General Bootes is closed to Will Robinson's ideas and strategies. Will Robinson feels that he has valuable information to share, information obtained through the torture of BLR leaders captured during the raids on the smaller bases. General Bootes seems disinterested and preoccupied. All signs suggest this will be the shortest war he has ever been involved with.

Congratulating Will Robinson for the work he has accomplished, General Bootes suggests his lack of battle experience makes his further participation useless. He tells Will Robinson, "You had the BLR on their heels. then you stopped pursuing them for two days, giving them time to regroup."

Will Robinson tries to explain, "Sir, we aren't the only ones bringing troops to this planet. The BLR have begun arriving; it appears they're going to fight us."

"*Good*," replies General Bootes, almost shouting. "We'll wipe them out in two days! Since you've unwisely delayed things, we may as well wait for the Altairians to arrive. I've got a score to settle with them; we'll send them in first."

When General Bootes was thirteen, his family vacationed on Altair. He and his brother were fishing from a boat when five older Altairian youths arrived on shore. They had fireworks resembling bottle rockets and roman candles and began aiming them at the boat. General Bootes and his brother panicked causing the boat to capsize. General Bootes resurfaced to find all the fishing gear was gone. His brother never resurfaced.

The BLR has successfully begun attacking some of the allied planets with troops headed to Earth. Altair, Becrux, and Adhara all sustained extensive damage with heavy casualties to their armies. Their forces headed to Earth have aborted and are returning to their home planets. The BLR fared better but lost valuable troops and equipment.

General Bootes has Gray troops moving in on the western BLR headquarters. They are staging four miles to the south. "Where are those good for nothing Altairians?" the general asks moments before being informed they and several other planets have aborted and are returning home. "Very well," he states before giving the order to attack.

As Will Robinson stated, BLR troops have been arriving on Earth. The western headquarters received several armies of reinforcements and are well prepared for battle.

Following a light shock-and-awe campaign by their fighter craft, the Grays advance. They move into an ambush and are badly beaten. They retreat with very little fight.

General Bootes rants and raves and asks, "Where did all those BLR come from?"

Will Robinson remains quiet until the general has calmed down, then tries to recommend another plan. The general has already come up with another plan and does not listen. "We'll wait a couple of days for reinforcements to arrive," he says.

Nybo, Ursa, Tiny, and the nuns are headed to a small BLR base in Chicago. They are stuck in traffic and hardly moving. Looking at a greenish river, Sister Agnes asks, "Why is the water so dirty?"

"Not just the water," replies Sister Anna, "Trash and dirt are everywhere. Even the air is dirty."

"It's called progress," says Tiny.

"I'm glad Deltoiga doesn't have progress," states Sister Angela. They arrive at the BLR base to find it has been destroyed.

A squadron of fighter craft from Epsilon has arrived. They are superior to BLR and all other fighter craft. They immediately engage BLR fighter craft in an air battle. The BLR sustain heavy damage in the fight.

General Bootes sends troops to attack the western BLR headquarters, and once again, they meet an ambush. Though they are better prepared, a retreat occurs after heavy casualties on both sides.

As the Grays retreat, the BLR pursue them. General Bootes had anticipated this possibility and a massive army is waiting. The BLR troops rush into a massacre. BLR fighter craft arrive, allowing approximately forty percent of their troops to escape. The fighter craft from Epsilon arrive and the BLR sustain heavy losses.

Things are no better for the eastern BLR headquarters. General Canopus directs the BLR forces in that battle. Though far outnumbered, the eastern BLR troops are holding their own; but with the casualties of each battle, their effectiveness and morale diminish.

King Alpha receives several updates daily. Assured things are going well and that the end is in sight, he decides to take a vacation to the planet Hadar, a Gray outpost in the northwest sector. King Alpha chooses not to receive updates for a day and a half, just as things begin taking a turn for the worse.

General Bootes is confident of victory over the BLR and relates his plan for the battle with the Earthlings. "First," he says, "we unleash some nonnuclear electromagnetic pulses to disrupt their communications."

Will Robinson explains, "Sir, our bases here on Earth have become dependent on the inferior technology utilized by the Earthlings.

General Bootes again refuses to listen, believing the technology possessed by the Grays can overcome anything. "Why would we mess around with inferior technology?" he asks.

General Bootes is fed up with Will Robinson and relocates him to the war in the east. Upset and under protest, Will Robinson heads east. Feeling relieved that Will Robinson is gone, General Bootes puts his feet on his desk. He is planning a massive invasion of the western BLR headquarters which should bring an end to this battle. The fighter craft from Epsilon will perform two days of bombing and destruction, followed by a massive invasion of ground troops.

With smug assuredness that the Grays have already won, he continues planning for the next step, the execution and enslavement of Earthlings. Snow begins falling bringing a smile to the general's face.

Nybo, Ursa, Tiny, and the nuns are tired of driving after missing the last scheduled stop at the destroyed BLR base. They approach another small base in northern Indiana, where they are greeted by a handful of BLR members, mostly scientist and doctors. "Where is everyone?" asks Tiny.

Someone responds, "They have all gone to the eastern headquarters to reinforce the troops there. The war isn't going well, I'm afraid. You all look tired, and you must be hungry. Come and join us for dinner. Our resources are getting low. All we can offer you is spaghetti."

Early in the meal, the discussion is pleasant, and the spaghetti disappears rapidly. The scientist and doctors have heard of Nybo and congratulate him on his daring mission that disrupted the Grays' transportation system. Nybo smiles with pride and points out that Ursa deserves credit also. Nybo's proud feeling evaporates as the discussion turns to the war.

One of the scientists, Dr. Beaker, relates, "I'm afraid there are few good reports; things are looking grim. It appears we won't be able to hold out much longer without reinforcements. Reports state only the Grays and their allies have troops headed here. The west could fall within a week; the east will fall shortly after."

Nybo asks, "Have you heard any news of Pamuhl, the Deltoigan voyager who is attempting to fly through the chaos in space? She should be well on her way to Deltoiga by now."

The scientist and doctors look at each other while Nybo continues. "Is Zeta still at the safe house in Arizona?"

After a pause, Dr. Beaker solemnly states, "Oh my. I guess you haven't heard. We intercepted a Gray report that the spacecraft was destroyed along with everyone in it. Zeta never reported to the safe house. If he's still alive, his whereabouts are unknown."

Nybo, who was thoroughly enjoying his meal, can no longer eat. Heartbroken, he thinks of Pamuhl and mumbles her nickname, "Spaghetti."

Dr. Beaker responds, "Oh, you want more."

General Auriga's diversion plan is put into action. By a stroke of luck, it involves Hadar. On Earth, there is a sudden change of luck for the BLR, giving them a needed morale boost.

CHAPTER 25

TURNING POINTS

The Grays' intelligence detects a large fleet of spacecraft headed toward Hadar. After annihilating Vega, the troops from the north sector were sent to Earth, leaving the area vulnerable. The leadership of the Grays are uncertain where the fleet of spacecraft are coming from. King Alpha could be in jeopardy. Troops must be sent to his defense immediately.

The Grays' reinforcements headed to Earth are redirected to the north sector, many of them had come from there. Manpower is pulled from the supply line on Alpha Centauri and is replaced by forced labor from nearby planets.

The king recently levied a war tax, upsetting the allied planets. They began withholding resources, arms and manpower which were pledged prior to the start of the war. The allied planets are now being asked to send the promised reinforcements to Earth but are not willing to weaken their own defenses resulting in perfunctory numbers being sent.

On Earth, the western BLR recognize it is a matter of days before they can no longer hold out. General Bootes decision to stop the battle while waiting for reinforcements has given the western BLR valuable time to rest and regroup.

General Bootes becomes extremely angry upon learning the reinforcements from Betelgeuse and Rigel are no longer in route to Earth. Hearing the paltry number of reinforcements being sent by the allied planets, he lifts a chair, walks over to his desk, and slams the chair down causing it to shatter. Wood splinters and papers fill the room. Still holding a chair leg, he beats it on the desk several times. Turning to his officers he rashly orders, "Tell the Epsilon fighter craft they're to attack at once!"

Nybo, Ursa, and Tiny wish to join the war. "We can't bring the nuns to eastern headquarters," says Ursa.

Dr. Beaker points out, "You were sent here to avoid the war."

Tiny states, "The potential war. They were sent here to avoid the potential war. Now there's a war and the BLR needs manpower."

Nybo states, "I'm responsible for my fellow Deltoigans and am on a quest to find Jous; but my desire is to join the war and destroy the Grays."

Dr. Beaker suggest Nybo talk to Father Ahmen at the catholic church near the base. "He's BLR; and we have a storage facility under the church. It's possible he might agree to house the nuns until you return."

Arrangements are made and the Deltoigan nuns are living at the church. The van is left there as part of the agreement. Nybo, Ursa, and tiny are headed to eastern BLR headquarters in an old jalopy belonging to the BLR.

The feast on Yinyang resembles a wedding reception. There's duckling and chicken, as well as a prize calf slaughtered special for the guest. Everyone is dressed in their best attire. There's music and dancing. A special dance is performed for the guest by Yinyang's most beautiful women. Everyone drinks more than their share of vino.

Pabloba listens as Zeta and Pamuhl relate their stories. They conclude telling him about the Grays and the fear of a war breaking out on Earth.

Pabloba tells them, "We have heard of an evil force in the third dimension. There's fear they would find their way to the Third and a half dimension, bringing their evil ways and enslaving our planets."

Pabloba relates how the dark side of Yinyang has attacked the good side of the planet over and over throughout history. "There have been times when our faith was weak, and our armies did not fare so well. When our faith is strong, Dog has fought with us. His armies are unbeatable. The planet has been in a constant state of flux."

The feast goes well into the night, and although they get little sleep, Pamuhl and Zeta find themselves well rested in the morning. Preparing to depart Yinyang, Pamuhl tells Zeta," You know I'm going to miss the Yinyangites. They remind me of blurry Deltoigans."

Following a breakfast resembling a banquet, they head to the spacecraft, shadowed by a long trail of Yinyangites. After countless goodbyes and hugs, the spacecraft takes flight and heads to Mir.

During the flight, Pamuhl states, "You know, you never told me how you became a member of the BLR."

Zeta says, "Sorry, I tend to get a little broken up whenever I think about my entire race being exterminated."

Pamuhl softly says, "I'm terribly sorry about that. I can't image what it would be like to return to Deltoiga and find it vanished."

Zeta responds, "That's why we need to stop the Grays. The fate of every planet everywhere is at stake. Perhaps even Yinyang and Mir."

Zeta continues his story. "So my great-great-grandfather, Abuelo, tried to resettle on other planets but was constantly hounded by the Grays. It isn't clear how he ended up on Earth, but it was the first place where he was left alone. He eventually met other aliens and they formed their own community. Years later, after his death it was found that his efforts to form an alliance against the Grays materialized into what was called the Black League Resistance. The alien community on Earth adopted the name for themselves."

It is a busy time at the safe house in Minneapolis. There is a record number of abductees being dumped in the area. Moe, Joe, and Cindy thought they were given an easy gig but find themselves working up to twenty hours some days. Star is completing training and ready to begin.

The north shore of Lake Superior is a UFO magnet. It has an extensive range of iron, a necessity for the Grays' diet while in Earth's atmosphere. Iron is shipped to Gray bases throughout the country but is currently at a standstill with the transport system down. There is a large underground base there, and a training camp for mutant warriors. The locals often report strange things happening in the area.

Defectors from the Grays are brought to the safe house. The defectors come from all planets. Some are from planets the BLR has never heard of. The defectors have been mutated to become half Gray.

Like Ursa, the fortunate ones retained enough of their native brain cells to recognize the evil perpetrated by the Grays. After enough abusive treatment, they flee when given the opportunity. Once cleansed, the defectors are sent to eastern BLR headquarters to join in the war.

A band of eight Gray Devils drive by the church and spot the van parked in front. They rush into the church with two of them who had a Catholic upbringing stopping to genuflect and make the sign of the cross. They are loud and screaming, beating their hands against the pews.

Father Ahmen emerges from a door next to the alter. While the chaos continues, he stops and genuflects toward Jesus hanging on the cross. After performing the sign of the cross, he turns toward the gang and says, "I'm Father Ahmen. How can I help you?"

The leader replies, "You can save your amen. We don't go for that pray to God crap."

The Gray Devils become quiet, and after spitting on the floor, the leader asks, "Where are they?"

Father Ahmen calmly replies, "Ah, you are referring to the new nuns."

One of the gang members throws a Bible across the church and says, "Some friends of ours said they're very special and recommended we talk to them."

Father Ahmen is overwhelmingly charismatic. People are drawn to him, as his presence brings calmness to anyone around him. Within seconds, the Gray Devils begin to feel the calmness he exudes. Father Ahmen tells them, "I can arrange for you to talk to them. It's getting late. You must be hungry. Come and dine with me, and afterward, we'll talk with the nuns."

Reluctantly, the Gray Devils agree. While eating spaghetti and listening to Father Ahmen talk about the salvation he has found through his belief in Jesus Christ, something odd happens to the gang. They begin asking questions about Jesus and faith. Father Ahmen gives each of them a Bible. After dinner an impromptu Bible study takes place, and the gang has forgotten about the nuns

The Bible study continues deep into the night. Father Ahmen insists they spend the night. When they arise late in the morning the Gray Devils all agree that this is what has been missing from their lives. During breakfast they ask Father Ahmen to baptize them and allow them to join his parish. Afterward, they meet the nuns and apologize for pursuing them. The nuns have no idea what they are talking about.

The fighter craft from Epsilon begin attacking the western BLR headquarters while the Gray troops prepare for the finale battle. Things are going as General Bootes had planned. He would have preferred having the diverted reinforcements to

create a massive overwhelming army, but the troops he has will be more than enough. In a few days, the western BLR will be defeated and the Gray army will head east to finish the war. Then it is on to the Earthlings.

CHAPTER 26

THERE IS STILL HOPE

King Alpha meets with the leaders of Hadar who are concerned about the security of their planet. They are alarmed about the destruction of Vega and the lack of Gray army defenses remaining in the north sector. The king assures them Vega had to be destroyed. He falsely tells them Vega was putting together an alliance to attack Hadar and other planets in the north. He then relates that within a couple of days, the Earth situation will be resolved and the Gray armies will return north to explore and expand their realm.

The king engages in a game of *sinnet* before cocktails and a nap. Sinnet can best be described as fast-paced tennis. The king is less than mediocre at the game but has only lost once. His opponent was executed after the game. No one would be foolish enough to beat the king, although most of his opponents could.

Upon awakening from his nap, the king is informed that the BLR on Earth are still fighting. He is told about the mysterious squadron of spacecraft headed toward Hadar. He orders the Gray reinforcements in route to Earth to be redirected to meet the mystery squadron.

The generals dare not tell him this is already happening. They praise the king for his decisiveness. Returning to Betelgeuse would be risky; but the Gray fighter craft should arrive in plenty of time to engage the mystery squadron before it reaches Hadar. The king is angry and ready to have someone executed until he is convinced it will be good public relations for him to lead a battle. This is certain to be a small skirmish with a guaranteed victory.

On Alpha Centauri, the forced labor is doing what it can to slow down and interrupt the supply line. Intentional errors are being made. Items are mislabeled or being transferred from the appropriately labeled box to a box labeled something else. Things are being shipped to the wrong location causing confusion and shortages on certain ammunition, along with delays on equipment maintenance.

As ordered, the Epsilon fighter craft begin attacking the western BLR headquarters. The BLR forces fight back vigorously but are outmatched. At the end of the day, the BLR casualties are heavy. Their fighter craft force has diminished to nominal numbers. In another day, the Gray army will move in and end the battle. There are to be no prisoners.

The BLR send their remaining fighter craft into what is certain to be the final battle. Their pilots are aware they are on a suicide mission but will fight to the end. Engaging the Epsilon fighter craft, they find something different about this battle.

The fighter craft from Epsilon are not maneuvering as swiftly as the day before. The density of Earth's atmosphere is heavier than anything they have ever flown in; it has taken its toll on the mechanisms of Epsilon's fighter craft.

The Epsilon fighter craft have operated at full capacity to fight the resistance created by the atmosphere and have required constant maintenance. Parts are becoming scarce and several of the new parts arriving are not correct. The snow adds extra drag, and the moisture affects fuel performance. BLR pilots are reporting that several Epsilon fighter craft are falling from the sky without being shot at.

Nybo, Ursa, and Tiny have arrived at the eastern BLR headquarters and are given a bleak briefing of the war by General Canopus. Upon learning of Nybo's voyager experience, General Canopus invites him to test fly a fighter craft. Looping, spinning, diving, and dipping, Nybo has a great time and forgets about the war for a moment. With a wide smile, Nybo volunteers to fly a fighter craft in the next battle.

The general explains that a fighter craft pilot is the most dangerous job in the war because of the superiority of the Epsilon fighter craft. The current life expectancy is about forty-five minutes.

Nybo ignores the warning and is granted his wish. Ursa insists she go along with him. "If he dies, I'm dying with him," she states.

After much debate, she will be allowed to go. Though not verbalized, the logic behind the decision is that within a week the BLR will likely be defeated, without survivors.

Pamuhl and Zeta land their spacecraft on Mir. Exiting the craft, a strange familiar feeling occurs. The planet looks exactly like Yinyang. Walking to a blurry banana fruit tree, Pamuhl reaches for one and misses on the first attempt. A blurry orange lake looks exactly like the one on Yinyang. They roast blurry banana fruit over a blurry fire near the lake and spend the night under the stars.

In the morning, they pick a dozen blurry bananas and start heading to the spacecraft. They are met by a blurry, four-and-a-half-foot, blue-haired, green-eyed man wearing a black robe and holding a staff. Looking around they notice other blue-haired, green-eyed, long-nosed people wearing black robes have joined them. "Welcome to Mir. I'm Bapablo," says the man. "We were informed you were coming my third dimensional friends. Come along."

"What's this place," asks Pamuhl. "It's exactly like Yinyang."

Bapablo explains, "You've landed on a small area of the planet where strange things happen. It's unknown why, but you get the feeling you've been here before. We call this place Déjà Vu. Once we walk over the hill, we'll be away from it. Seems like I was here only yesterday."

Upon reaching the top of the hill, Pamuhl and Zeta look out onto a beautiful blurry city. Large blurry buildings colored gold and silver, all sparkling in the sunshine. "This is amazing," says Pamuhl.

They are taken to the municipal building and introduced to the city leaders, and to the czar of Mir, Czar Bubelli. Meeting with the czar, they tell the story of their journey into deep space and how they arrived on Mir.

Pamuhl tells the czar they are trying to find their way back to the third dimension and to Deltoiga. She explains the Grays have visited Deltoiga. "My planet must be convinced of the true intensions of the Grays," she says.

After hearing their story, the czar gives them their first news of the war on Earth. The Czar states, "On Mir, we are aware of the aggressive nature of the Grays. There's news of the third-dimensional place called Earth where a war is in progress between a group called the BLR and the Grays."

Zeta tells the czar, "I'm of the BLR."

Pamuhl says, "He's the one who saved me."

The czar continues. "The news isn't good. Although the BLR has done damage to many of the Grays' allied planets, the war on Earth appears fruitless." A hopeless, sick feeling overtakes Pamuhl and Zeta.

The czar tells them about Vega being destroyed. "Vega was Mir's allied planet in the third dimension. They had warned us about the Grays before their planet was demolished. Had the Grays not been so hasty with Vega, they would have found their way to the third and a half dimension. We have developed a weapon for use in the third dimension, which we were about to give to Vega before it was shattered to pieces. Enough of bad news, let's prepare for the banquet."

In the evening, there is a grand banquet. Just as they did on Yinyang, the attendees are dressed in their best attire. There's music and dancing. Delicious food and drink are served. Pamuhl tells Zeta she is torn between helping Earth and returning to Deltoiga. "I have to warn my planet," she says, "I must go to Deltoiga."

Zeta explains to her, "I understand how you feel but consider this: If the BLR is defeated on Earth, it won't be long before the Grays occupy Deltoiga. Choosing to warn Deltoiga rather than returning to Earth to fight will only postpone the inevitable. The Grays must be defeated."

After conversing throughout the night, Czar Bubelli feels he can trust Pamhul and Zeta. As they bid each other good night, the Czar says, "Come to my office in the morning, I believe we may be able to help."

Following breakfast, Pamuhl and Zeta meet with the czar. After giving directions for returning to the third dimension, the czar states, "Your spacecraft is being outfitted with a vibrator bomb gun."

Pamuhl feels violated by not having been consulted about it and says with shock in her voice, "Wait! What?"

The czar explains, "I mentioned to you yesterday that we had developed a weapon for use in the third dimension. With the demolition of Vega, we now recognize the necessity of bringing down the Grays before they discover the third-and-a-half dimension."

He then produces something resembling a short twenty-two caliber cartridge. Holding it between his thumb and forefinger, he lifts his hand into the air. "Here it is," he states with pride.

Zeta excitedly states, "What's this? You build up our hope and give us this! We're not at war with squirrels."

"Keep your voice down," says the czar. "We don't want this thing going off."

Pamuhl asks, "What's that thing going to do?"

Czar Bubelli feels insulted while telling them, "This is capable of destroying half the planet. Upon impact, a vibration is released, so intense no living thing can survive it. There isn't a material in existence that can withstand its effects. Even if you shoot and miss your target, it will detonate and cause mortal damage to things within the specified range."

"Including us," interrupts Pamuhl.

Czar Bubelli grows impatient. "Do you want our help or not?"

Zeta points at the cartridge. "Yes, but you are asking us to trust our lives to that. It's hard to believe you want us to go to battle with a BB gun."

The czar responds, "A simple thank-you would be enough. Your spacecraft is also being outfitted with an anti-bad-vibe deflector shield. In the event a cartridge detonates near your craft, you'll be protected. Take this very seriously. This weapon can do massive destruction. You lock in your target and pull a trigger. The range and field are automatically determined. It's very simple to use."

On Earth, Will Robinson receives a report of a tall woman and short man joining the eastern BLR troops. The Deltoigans had described to Will Robinson the human form taken by Nybo. Will Robinson suddenly recalls that Deltoigans are capable of changing form and deducts, "Of course! The little Deltoigan SOB can change form. He's Dr. Chu!"

CHAPTER 27

THE VIBRATOR BOMB IS TESTED

King Alpha takes charge of the upcoming battle with the mystery squadron. The defenses on Hadar are on red alert as their fighter craft jump into action. The Grays' Fighter craft unite with them forming a mass of destruction. The mystery squadron is not swayed and continues advancing.

Fighter craft from Spica and Pollux are approaching the squadron from the east and west. The mystery squadron is not dissuaded and remains steadily on course. Pollux sends ground units to reinforce the troops of Hadar. It appears the battle may be larger than anticipated.

The mystery squadron is asked to identify themselves; there is no reply as they proceed forward. They are given a warning, then another; still no response as they reach the point where action becomes necessary.

King Alpha gives the order and the first wave of the mystery squadron is fired upon. Several of their craft burst into flames, while others spiral off into space. Oddly, the squadron does not attempt to maneuver or fight back but continues to advance, wave after wave.

One of the Grays' generals says, "They seem to be taunting us! We may need reinforcements!"

The king calls for reinforcements from Capella then transfers command to General Drago before retreating to an underground bunker. The second wave of the mystery squadron is attacked with the same result, no attempt to evade or retaliate. The squadron remains steadily on course.

The scenario continues for hours until the mystery squadron is almost destroyed. The Gray fighter craft pilots and their allies are exhausted and running out of ammunition. The remaining craft from the mystery squadron are rounded up and taken to Hadar. Once on the ground, they are surrounded by hordes of ground troops. King Alpha emerges from the underground bunker and retakes command. Reinforcements are arriving from several allied planets.

The king anticipates a moment of glory as he orders the pilots from the captured spacecraft to exit with their hands up. There is no response, so the king orders the pilots to be extracted.

Cautiously approaching each craft, the soldiers are in position. The first craft is opened, and a team of soldiers enter. In a moment, they exit and state, "There's no one in here and there aren't any weapons." The second craft is entered, and again, there is no pilot or weapons. The third, fourth, and fifth craft have the same result. The extraction continues for hours without a single pilot or weapon being found. The king is badly embarrassed, and four generals are ordered to be executed.

General Auriga had gone to allied planets and rounded up discarded and discontinued BLR spacecraft, anything that could be salvaged and made to fly. These were formed into a squadron and sent on a course to Hadar to divert the fighter craft of the Grays and their allies away from Earth. The plan worked perfectly and could not have happened at a better time, just as the Epsilon fighter craft were beginning to experience problems.

Pamuhl and Zeta are given a magnificent send-off and head for the third dimension. Their spacecraft armed with a vibrator bomb gun is now one of the most lethal weapons in space. As the spacecraft continues to proceed toward the third dimension, things become progressively less blurry.

Entering the third dimension, the two voyagers can see clearly and breathe a sigh of relief. They had both entertained the fear of never seeing clearly again. As they cheer and smile, Zeta observes, "It might take a while to get accustomed to seeing clearly."

Pamuhl has figured out the navigational system, and the spacecraft is headed to Earth. Pamuhl states, "I can't believe I was so close to returning to Deltoiga. Now I'll be back on Earth."

Zeta says, "First we have to make it to Earth. There are a lot of unfriendly craft between here and there."

The excitement of being in the third dimension is replaced by uncertainty. Will they have an encounter with the enemy before getting to Earth? What is happening on Earth? Will this BB gun of a weapon really work?

Three Gray spacecraft approach them. Zeta loads the vibrator bomb gun and takes aim. "Say hello to my little friend," he says quoting the line from *Scarface.*

"Just shoot," Pamuhl orders.

As promised, the weapon automatically determines the range, and a shot is fired. The vibrator bomb detonates, and two of the Grays' craft disintegrate. The third is sent violently spiraling off into space.

"Whew!" Pamuhl shouts. "You could put an eye out with one of those!"

Zeta states, "Those amazing scientists on Mir. They sure saved our bacon."

Pamuhl responds, "Let's get to Earth and eradicate some Grays."

A record number of minds are cleansed at the Minneapolis safe house. A double agent who sides with the BLR has been at the Grays' North Shore operation and reports they are planning to attack all BLR safe houses, beginning with the one in Minneapolis. All the staff are issued a SC2 spontaneous combustion gun, and a few reserve BLR troops are posted at the house, removing needed reinforcements from eastern headquarters.

Finishing a nineteen-hour day, the safe house staff retire to their beds. At one forty-five in the morning, a small army of Grays encroaches on the safe house. A BLR reservist is standing guard. He sees a flash racing toward him and looks down at his abdomen in shock as the flash penetrates him. He sees smoke rising from the wound before he disappears. A second reservist comes to relieve the vanished sentry and meets the same fate.

Star is restless and unable to sleep. Her mind is racing as item after item from her training pops into her head. She steps out of bed and wonders if she did the right thing riding along with Moe, Joe, and Cindy. *I saw right away that there was something off about them. Why didn't I leave when Moe had first seen me and pulled the car over to yell at Joe? Because I love Joe, that's why.* She walks to the window and, looking outside, notices a flash zooming across the yard. Witnessing the flash strike a sentry, she observes smoke rising from the sentry's midsection and sees him vanish. She sees Gray soldiers moving toward the house.

Distraught and afraid, she stands next to the window, shaking and barely able to stand. She attempts to yell warnings to the others, but her voice is frozen. Violently shaking, she manages to move toward the bed where Joe is soundly sleeping. Within a few steps of the bed, her legs give out, so she lunges, falling short. Her outstretched arm slaps down on Joe who breathes with a grunt and rolls over.

Star finds the strength to rise to all fours and crawl to the bed. Grabbing Joe and feebly shaking him, she attempts to shout wake up but can barely produce a whisper. Fear increases as her body gets a sudden burst of adrenaline, and she shakes Joe more vigorously.

Awakening, Joe groggily inquires, "What?"

Star is still in shock and points toward the window with a shaking hand while yelling in a barely audible whisper, "There, there, over there."

With eyes half shut and his brain in a fog, Joe asks," What? What is it?"

Star is grabbing and pulling Joe with one shaky hand while pointing at the window with the other shaking hand. Joe begins to gain consciousness and sits up on the bed. Seeing the terror on Star's face, he jumps out of bed. "What is it?" he asks with fright. Star continues to point at the window with a shaking hand.

Joe rushes to the window but does not see anything. "What is it?" he asks, continuing to look.

Turning to walk back to the bed and comfort Star, he catches a glimpse of movement outside. He observes two Gray soldiers rushing toward the house. He rushes to wake the others, and he grabs his SC2. Cindy runs through the house, waking and warning everyone.

Joe fires his SC2, and a Gray soldier disintegrates. Moe runs to another window and begins shooting. "We need more light," states Moe.

Joe reduces the power of his SC2 and shoots a Gray soldier, causing him to spontaneously combust and burst into flames rather than to disintegrate. He shoots another, and there is a second burning Gray in the yard. A third Gray is ignited, and the burning soldiers act as torches, lighting up the yard.

Moe and Joe shoot soldier after soldier. Cindy returns and joins them with her SC2. Star has regained composure and heads toward the window to join Joe. She stumbles and falls. Joe goes to her and assists her up. A flash comes through the window headed for Joe. He bends over to retrieve Star's SC2, and the flash flies over him, striking Star causing her to vanish. Joe straightens up and turns to hand Star her weapon. "Where did she go?" he asks.

Joe's heart sinks as he realizes what has happened. Standing and staring at the floor with a broken heart, he hears Moe say, "Joe! A little help."

Joe fills with anger as his mind becomes focused on revenge. He returns to the window with a SC2 in each hand and begins wildly firing.

A commotion breaks out on the main floor as Grays have entered the house. Crossfire ensues and members from both sides are disintegrated. Gray soldiers continue to enter the house, forcing the BLR to retreat to the upper level. Kappa throws a small concussion bomb onto the main floor. The entire house shakes when the bomb detonates. Afterward, incapacitated Gray soldiers are lying on the floor, waiting to be disintegrated. The remaining Gray soldiers retreat.

The battle is over. Joe sits on the floor and stares blankly at the spot where Star evaporated. Moe places his hand on Joe's shoulder and says comforting words. Joe hears mumbling but is incapable of comprehending anything. He looks up at Moe causing him to take a step back.

His eyes frighten Moe. They are blank and appear almost black with evil. They reveal Joe is on a mission for blood and death.

The BLR survivors gather on what is left of the ground floor. Kappa and a few of the others make plans to convert the stunned Gray soldiers lying on the floor into BLR soldiers. Joe descends the stairs and immediately begins shooting the lifeless Grays. "Stop!" orders Kappa.

Joe looks at him and Kappa's eyes widen as he steps back with his arms extended forward to keep Joe away. Kappa had seen the same face Moe had seen. Joe continues shooting until the last Gray has vanished.

CHAPTER 28

NYBO VERSUS WILL ROBINSON

Nybo prepares to fly into his first battle. Listening to other pilots speak, he realizes the success rate is low and the chances for survival are lower. Sitting quietly, he pictures various battle scenarios in his mind. His heart meets his stomach, producing adrenaline that his body attempts to control.

Walking outside, he begins to feel an array of emotions. Fighting against Epsilon fighter craft is futile. *I'm not likely to survive*, he thinks as his heart sinks. Adrenaline rushes through his body. *I must go. They killed Pamuhl and Fraxel.* Ursa comes to the front of his thoughts and his heart fills with love and joy that is quickly extinguished with grief as realizes he will be responsible for her death. Snow begins to fall as he enters the building.

Ursa would not listen to the barrage of pleas asking her to remain behind. She is adamant about being with Nybo. The only way to pry her away from Nybo is to give her a fighter craft of her own. She has begun taking flying lessons.

Following the dismantling of the Minneapolis safe house, Moe, Joe, and Cindy are on their way to eastern headquarters. Joe is full of vengeance and ready to fight. A trigger went off when Star was disintegrated, and getting even is his only focus. He is prepared to take on the entire Gray army.

The Gray Devils have formed a small army of their own, which is headed east, determined on getting vengeance from the Indian and the nuns. Father Ahmen has used church funds to customize the van, which now displays the church's name, Saint Bernard, along with images of Jesus Christ and the Mother Mary. The license plate was discarded and a new one reads LETSPRAY.

Epsilon fighter pilots are about to assault the BLR eastern headquarters. But when the order is given to enter the craft, there is a sudden shortage of pilots. Just as Earth's atmosphere has taken its toll on the fighter craft in the west, the environment is beginning to affect the pilots themselves. Several have fallen ill and are unable to continue in battle.

Will Robinson is angry and becoming irrational. He insists he can fly anything. He enters one of the Epsilon fighter craft and the reduced fleet takes to the air.

The BLR pilots are ordered to their fighter craft. Nybo turns to Ursa and gives a final plea for her to stay. His plea is cut short by the look Ursa shoots at him. They enter the craft and are on their way to the upper edge of Earth's atmosphere.

Epsilon's fighter craft are reaching battle altitude. Will Robinson is lagging. Being inexperienced with Epsilon fighter craft, he practices maneuvers. Snow begins to fall as his craft gains altitude and crosses paths with a commercial airline flight en route to Las Vegas. The passengers have all qualified to compete in a contest titled America's Luckiest Person. Irrationally deciding to take a practice shot, Will Robinson shoots, and following a burst of flames, the commercial plane vanishes along with 237 unlucky passengers.

The BLR Fighter craft fall into a string of box formations, where two craft are side by side followed by two other craft forming a box. The strategy is to have the front two craft split and have the following two craft shoot at fighters pursuing them. Nybo is in a rearward craft and prepared to shoot.

A BLR fighter craft near Nybo bursts into flames as the battle begins. The two forward craft split, giving Nybo an opportunity to shoot. Without time to think, he shoots and misses. He witnesses another BLR fighter craft burst into flames. Nybo repeatedly fires shots and misses. The Epsilon fighter craft are too fast and agile, side slipping and barrel rolling. They seem impossible to hit. The chaos increases as the sky fills with smoke while fighter craft and bullets are flying in all directions.

Ursa has one hand on Nybo's leg and one hand covering her eyes. Nybo makes a successful shot and joyfully states, "Got one!" Ursa removes her hand from her eyes. Another BLR fighter craft burst into flames followed by an Epsilon fighter craft. After another successful shot, Nybo states, "Now I'm getting it!" Ursa claps.

The number of BLR craft diminishes as Nybo joins in a box formation. Flying one of the forward craft, he is intimidated by an approaching line of Epsilon craft. As shots are fired at him, he prepares to split. The BLR craft flying next to him is hit and bursts into flame. There is a reverberation, causing Nybo to lose control of his craft and spiral down toward Earth. He unsuccessfully fights to regain control of the disheveled craft. The runaway craft rips the clouds, and Nybo finds himself in a snowstorm, which adds to the confusion.

Ursa asks, "Are we going to crash?"

In all the confusion, Nybo had forgotten Ursa was there. The scared emotion he is experiencing jumps a notch. Regaining composure, he gets a burst of adrenaline as he realizes he must save Ursa.

The craft glows red as warning light after warning light flashes. Nybo puts the systems into override to bypass normal channels that are no longer functioning. He engages the speed brake, attempting to slow the craft. A gear box begins to smoke, making breathing difficult.

As Nybo waves his hand in front of his eyes, attempting to clear the smoke, he hears Ursa cough. He tightly grips the steering stick as it fights everything he tries to do. The gyroscope spins like a top. The heavy snow makes it impossible to distinguish up from down.

The speed brake begins to gain control as the craft slows. A crack and buzz are heard as the speed brake overheats and a wire catches fire. The craft smells like an electrical fire.

The vertical stabilizer levels the craft. Using the rudder and body flaps, Nybo steadies the craft. He wipes the tears from Ursa's eyes and gives her a comforting hug.

Collecting his composure, Nybo begins to ascend, hoping to rejoin the battle. From the thick wall of snow, an Epsilon fighter craft materializes. Nybo fires several unsuccessful shots. The opposing craft begins firing at Nybo and Ursa.

Drawing from his limited repertoire, Nybo maneuvers his way through the attack. The two craft nearly collide, passing each other. Will Robinson, the Epsilon fighter craft pilot, manages to catch a glimpse of a short fat man and a tall woman. "No way," he mutters to himself, recognizing them.

In the battle above, Epsilon pilots are beginning to experience a decline in the performance of their craft, leveling the playing field for the BLR. Duplicating the experience of the western fleet, overworked mechanisms are failing, and diluted fuel is causing hesitation and even stalling. Several of the Epsilon craft are falling from the sky without being shot.

Below the clouds, Will Robinson and Nybo make several passes at each other, firing multiple rounds unsuccessfully. Nybo suddenly realizes his ammunition supply is dwindling. As the craft pass each other once again, Nybo fires his final shot. Nybo dips, dives, and rolls, maneuvering his craft out of the line of fire. Will Robinson soon realizes his craft is faster and more agile than Nybo's.

After a short pursuit, Will Robinson has Nybo and Ursa in his sights. Locking in on their craft, he prepares to take the kill shot. "Here is what fat little Deltoigan SOBs get when they screw with Grays," he says before shooting.

As he fires the shot, his craft hesitates, forcing him to miss. Nybo fruitlessly maneuvers as Will Robinson locks him in his sights again. "Hasta la vista, baby," he says as his craft does a double hesitation.

The Epsilon craft quickly regains a favorable position for locking in another shot attempt. Will Robinson decides no messing around this time. Nybo and Ursa exchange final goodbyes as the death craft lines up behind them.

A sputter and hesitation occur as the Epsilon fighter craft stalls and falls to Earth. Nybo and Ursa are confused and unsure what is happening. After a long tense moment, they begin to relax. Nybo returns to the BLR base and is given the news of the positive turn of events.

Before long, the remaining BLR fleet return to base. A celebration erupts with laughing and champagne toasts. General Canopus enters the room and congratulates everyone.

"Enjoy the moment," he tells them before adding, "Two things. We have reports of Gray fighter craft coming from Hadar. They're joined by Pollux and Spica. Secondly, Gray troops are attacking western headquarters. There's little hope for their survival. The Gray troops here in the east are taking offensive positions. There's likely to be an attack within a day or two. Ready yourselves."

The vibrator bomb gun proves to be effective during a couple of skirmishes encountered by Pamuhl and Zeta as they approach Earth. Headed for the western headquarters, Pamuhl asks, "When we get near headquarters, how are they going to know we're on their side?"

Zeta responds, "I don't know."

The Gray army is getting closer and closer to the western BLR base with every new attack. A substantial portion of Epsilon's fighter craft are grounded. Those still operating are underperforming. The BLR fighter craft are holding the Gray army at bay. Both the BLR pilots and equipment need a break. Receiving news of the enemy fighter craft headed to Earth, the western headquarters teeters on surrender.

King Alpha returns to Betelgeuse. Everyone who can stays out of his way. The fighter craft from Hadar have joined the others headed to Earth.

The BLR forces in space patiently wait for the Hadar fighter craft to be en route a couple of days. Then the planet will be attacked.

CHAPTER 29

LIFE IN THE STONE AGE

Concerned over the disappearance of a commercial airliner, world leaders begin pointing their fingers at each other. There were no distress transmissions from the pilots. The strangest part of the mystery is there was no wreckage found, no black box.

International relationships are stretched to the breaking point. Blinded by their distrust for each other, world leaders fail to consider the possibility of alien involvement. Missiles are prepared for launching. Earth is now a fragile egg, waiting to be cracked by its own inhabitants.

The Gray army in the west begins advancing on BLR headquarters. The BLR soldiers had voted unanimously to fight to the death rather than surrender. The failure of the Epsilon fighter craft to carry out the two-day attack has allowed the BLR to reinforce their eroded defenses.

Moe, Joe, and Cindy arrive at the BLR eastern headquarters. They are still carrying their SC2 weapons. On their way to see General Canopus, they miss crossing paths with Nybo and Ursa by less than a minute.

General Canopus meets with them and learns the details of the Minneapolis safe house battle. He then informs them of the grim situation they are facing. "A battle could erupt at any moment. We are out manned and out armed," he explains.

Hovering in space, the Betelgeusian maximum-power battle craft awaits orders from the king. It is prepared to move into position and fulfill its purpose. On a whim, Earth could be destroyed, if its inhabitants do not destroy it first.

Pamuhl and Zeta miss crossing paths with the maximum-power battle craft by an hour. They are three hours ahead of crossing paths with the first wave of the Gray fleet headed to Earth.

The battle begins in the west. The first wave of Grays charges forward while a second wave advances from the rear. BLR troops are thin and running low on ammunition. They fight vigorously and hold their own. Suddenly, a seemingly endless wave of Grays appears. The heart of every BLR soldier sinks as they realize this will be the end. They had decided to fight till death and that is what they will do.

Pamuhl and Zeta approach the western BLR headquarters and see the attack taking place. "Load one up," says Pamuhl.

Zeta places a cartridge into the weapon. "I'll restrict the field as best I can," he says.

Taking aim, he fires a shot into the Gray army. The bomb detonates leaving a hole in the middle of the advancing soldiers. The remaining soldiers are stunned. They freeze for a moment and then retreat. Within a few moments, the entire Gray army has retreated.

A round of cheers explodes as Pamuhl and Zeta exit the spacecraft. Awestruck by the devastation that headquarters has taken, they ask, "What has been happening? It's amazing anyone is still alive." Tales of various battles are related to them as they are escorted to meet Major Canis.

General Bootes is furious. Panicked that King Alpha will hear of his failure, he orders Earth's satellites destroyed. Within hours, the maximum-power battle craft moves into position and releases several electromagnetic pulses, flinging Earth back into the stone age.

World leaders blame each other for the blackout and order missiles to be launched. They quickly learn it is not possible. The first wave of Gray fighter craft headed to Earth are impacted by the electromagnetic pulses and now float aimlessly in space, buying time for the BLR.

General Bootes had been right about one thing, the superior technology of the Grays. Utilizing the maximum-power battle craft as a relay, communication with Betelgeuse occurs. King Alpha learns of the defeat and orders General Bootes be escorted back to Betelgeuse. The king orders all Gray troops be evacuated. He has the maximum-power battle craft move into position and prepare for the destruction of Earth.

General Uranus convinces the king that victory over Earth can still be achieved. General Uranus tells him, "The Grays' fleet of fighter craft are beginning to arrive in the east. Our troops are in position to attack. We can do battle tomorrow and have victory by the end of the day. Then we head west and finish it."

The king asks, "Do you really believe we can pull it out, Uranus?"

The general guarantees it.

A meeting occurs between Pamuhl, Zeta, and Major Canis. The major elatedly inquires about the vibration bomb gun. Pamuhl and Zeta relate their tale for over an hour. Major Canis congratulates them on their timing and informs them the fight is over for the western BLR. He explains that they no longer have enough ammunition to go through another battle. The major tells them, "If you hadn't arrived when you did, we would have fallen. We were within minutes of the end."

Pamuhl asks about Nybo and the others. Major Canis informs them Nybo and the other Deltoigans have not been heard from since leaving the Mount Rushmore base. He then conveys the fate of the Minneapolis safe house. "A lot of lives were lost. We don't know who survived or where the survivors are."

Pamuhl utters, "Cindy. Those bass turds."

Surveillance indicates Gray troops in the west are withdrawing from Earth. BLR bases were constructed for the long run. Several alternate energy sources are utilized. Wind, solar, and hydropower are all employed. Methods have been developed for converting gases contained within the earth into energy. The BLR communication has been hampered but not eliminated. The east and west inform each other of their situations.

Earth is experiencing a worldwide blackout. Everyone in all nations are put under a curfew and ordered to remain in their homes. Peace is not experienced due to survival issues. People panic and rush out onto the streets and then become aggressive toward one another. Authorities have been preparing to deliver food, water, and necessities to the masses but are pulled away to deal with riots and shootings. Fires occur throughout the planet with no one to fight them.

Shops are looted as people fight over stolen items. Grocery stores are emptied. Pharmacies and hardware stores are demolished. Dead bodies lay in the streets as the authorities shoot the looters and the looters shoot each other. Autos are unable to move, as the streets are filled with stalled and incinerated cars. Burning gas stations gush flames high into the air.

The army of Gray Devils have run out of gas. They are stuck near the eastern BLR headquarters where a battle is about to break out. Gathered around a campfire they are approached by several soldiers. One of the soldiers asks them to identify themselves. "We are the Gray Devils," someone replies.

"Come with us," they are told and taken prisoner. As they are about to enter the interrogation room, one of them sees Nybo. "Hey, I know you," he says, pointing at Nybo.

Nybo recognizes him as the one who threw him into the dumpster. "Not you guys," he says.

"You know these guys?" asks the interrogation officer.

Nybo responds, "Know them, no, but we do have a history." After Nybo relates the incident from the gas station, the Gray Devils apologize.

Once convinced that the Gray Devils are not working with the Grays, the BLR recruits them and prepares them for the battle. Tiny sees the man he threw into the dumpster and says, "I thought I threw you away."

The battle is about to begin. The Grays fighter craft have arrived and begin attacking. Their ground troops begin to charge. The situation appears hopeless. General Uranus intends total elimination of the BLR. Moe, Joe, Cindy, Tiny, and the Gray Devils fight side by side.

Nybo and Ursa join the rest of the BLR fleet and are off to engage the Grays' fighter craft. The performance capabilities of the fighter craft utilized by the Grays and the BLR are similar. After fighting with the superior Epsilon fighter craft, the Grays' fighter craft seem to be in slow motion.

The BLR sustain some losses in the air battle but have forced the Gray fighter craft to retreat. BLR pilots prepare to return to base when a second wave of Gray fighter craft appear. The second wave is larger than the first. The air battle escalates. The BLR fleet continues to be successful but is beginning to dwindle in numbers. Ammunition is running low as a third wave of Gray fighter craft materialize.

Nybo uses the last of his ammunition and breaks away from the battle to head to base and reload. He suddenly finds himself flying toward a horde of Gray fighter craft. Maneuvering his craft, he stays just out of range. The Grays' craft are pursuing him when he notices his fuel is running low. He turns to Ursa and takes her hand. "I love you. Too bad we didn't have more time together." They give each other a farewell kiss.

Pamuhl and Zeta are on their way to the eastern base when they come upon the air war. Seeing a group of Gray fighter craft pursuing a lone BLR craft, Zeta fires a shot. The group of Gray fighter craft disintegrate. "We just saved that guy's bacon," remarks Pamuhl.

Feeling their fighter craft shake, Nybo unlocks from the kiss and sees there are no longer Gray fighter craft pursuing them. Confused, they return to base.

The remaining BLR fighter craft are low on fuel. Many are out of ammunition. The battle turns into target practice for the Gray pilots until their forces abruptly begin disappearing. The Gray pilots report that their fighter craft are vanishing a dozen at a time.

They retreat from the battle. Choosing not to pursue the fleeing Gray fighter craft, Pamuhl and Zeta turn their attention to the ground battle. After firing a couple of shots into the Gray army, their troops scatter and retreat.

The battle has ended. Pamuhl and Zeta arrive at the base and are treated like heroes. Nybo sees them, and he and Ursa rush to give them hugs. "We thought you were dead," says Nybo, beginning to cry.

The joy of the reunion brings tears to everyone's eyes. General Canopus arrives and announces that the Gray troops are leaving Earth. The exhausted pilots find the energy to celebrate.

King Alpha is given the bad news. He stomps around the room and says, "Get Uranus to Betelgeuse. I'll tear Uranus apart!" Things are about to get ugly for the Gray generals.

Pamuhl and Zeta inform Nybo and Ursa of the Minneapolis safe house battle. Fearing the worst, their hearts sink. Nybo says, "It's like I can hear their voices."

Joe passes by and sees them. He calls out, "Nybo, Ursa!"

Ursa says, "Yes, I can hear them too."

Joe runs over and grabs Nybo's shoulder. There are hugs and smiles as the group sees Joe. They are soon joined by Moe and Cindy. Laughing and celebrating, they relate their stories to each other.

That evening there is a grand celebration. The Gray Devils mingle with Nybo and Ursa. One of them says to Nybo, "You know, when we first met you at that gas station, you said, 'You have no idea who you are messing with.' You were right."

General Canopus joins the group and congratulates them. "Earth is saved for now," he says. "But they will just go somewhere else."

Nybo and Pamuhl give each other a concerned look as they both think of Deltoiga. The maximum-power battle craft is in position, awaiting orders.

In the morning, a meeting is held between Pamuhl, Zeta, General Canopus, and other BLR leaders. General Canopus begins by saying, "First, the good news. BLR troops in space have had successful campaigns on Hadar, Pollux, and Spica."

"Now the bad news. Pamuhl, you are flying one of the most devastating weapons known to anyone anywhere." Pamuhl smiles. General Canopus continues. "You have done a great service to the BLR and to free planets everywhere. But a difficult decision must be made."

Pamuhl responds, "What do you mean?"

The general replies, "No determination has been arrived at, but taking your spacecraft back to Deltoiga is out of the question."

Pamuhl asks, "How will I get there?"

The meeting is interrupted by news of the Betelgeusian maximum-power battle craft approaching Earth. The general states, "Pamuhl, we need you and Zeta to fly one more mission."

Pamuhl is disturbed by the meeting and experiencing a mixture of anger and anticipation as she prepares for the battle.

A small fleet of BLR fighter craft climb into Earth's atmosphere. They will serve as a distraction to allow Pamuhl and Zeta to approach the battle craft undetected. Zeta sees that Pamuhl is disturbed and reassures her that things will work themselves out. She remains quiet. They continue to focus on the meeting rather than the battle.

The BLR fighter craft perform exceptionally well, while Pamuhl and Zeta move into position.

Zeta says, "Lets crank this baby up and see what it can do."

A shot is fired utilizing the full-strength setting, causing the Betelgeusian maximum-power battle craft to explode and disappear. Their craft shakes violently from the repercussion, but they are saved by the anti-bad-vibe shield.

Being distracted before taking the shot caused them to overlook the safety of the BLR fighter craft in the battle. Over half are destroyed. The effects of the battle craft explosion is felt on Earth. There are earthquakes and tsunamis.

Pamuhl and Zeta return to Earth as heroes. The fate of the Deltoigan spacecraft is still undetermined.

King Alpha gathers his generals to determine the next conquest.

The inhabitants of Earth have begun to settle. There is no merchandise left to loot. Leaders begin to deliver food and necessities to the masses. Earth will begin to return to normal within a week. People are under curfew and remain in their homes without cellphones and television. Through all the chaos and stone-age conditions, people are experiencing peace on Earth.

OTHER BOOKS BY THE AUTHOR

Printed in the United States
By Bookmasters